D0429465

GOOD-BYE

and

AMEN

ALSO BY BETH GUTCHEON

GOOD-BYE

and

AMEN

BETH GUTCHEON

WILLIAM MORROW

An Imprint of HarperCollins*Publishers*

FIRST EDITION

Designed by Nicola Ferguson

Library of Congress Cataloging-in-Publication Data

Gutcheon, Beth Richardson.
   Good-bye and amen : a novel / Beth Gutcheon. — 1st ed.
     p.   cm.
   ISBN 978-0-06-053907-8
   1. Married people—Fiction.   2. Vacation homes—Fiction.
3. Maine—Fiction.   4. Domestic fiction.   I. Title.   II. Title:
Good-bye and amen.   III. Title: Good-bye and amen.

   PS3557.U844G66   2008
   813'.54—dc22   2008004256

08 09 10 11 12 WBC/RRD 10 9 8 7 6 5 4 3 2 1

For Ann Standish Mueller
Beloved Old Same

CONTENTS

· I ·
THE
LOTTERY

The trouble started when Jimmy took the piano.

Not their famous father's concert Steinway; that was too valuable to keep and was, anyway, nine feet long. Jimmy took the piano from the living room, the baby grand that had belonged to their Danish aunt Nina, the Resistance hero. Everyone knew Monica wanted that piano more than anything, and certainly more than Jimmy did.

Well, we all knew it. We assume Jimmy knew.

The middle-aged orphans' lottery. Three grown siblings come together at the scene of their shared childhood, which they experienced the same and totally differently in about equal parts, to divide up the contents of the house they grew up in. Was there ever a scene more fraught with possibility for bloodless injuries, sepsis in wounds no sane person wants to reopen? They'd have been better off burning the house down. But they hadn't. So few do.

Which we think is just as well. Birth is usually instructive. Death always. But as one of the minor passages, this one holds much interest. Deciding within a family how to divide or share what the dead leave behind is a test that tells.

In this family, Eleanor needs neither money nor things, but she likes to win, at least sometimes. And as eldest, feels entitled. Monica needs everything, and as middle and least-loved child, has her issues. And Jimmy as the youngest and well-known favorite feels ... well, it's often impossible to know what Jimmy feels. He's a stage-five thinker, to the surprise of a good many of us. We'd love to know if this came from his Buddhist period, or if it was all those psychedelic drugs.

Eleanor Moss Applegate We were in the dining room of the house in Connecticut. We grew up there, but none of us had lived there full-time since we were fifteen, forty years ago in my case. Jimmy did, here and there, whenever he was kicked out of school, but not for decades. Of course we visited our parents there, but Mother was pretty territorial. She didn't like people prowling, especially her grandchildren, so now that we had the run of the house, what was there came as a revelation. All our mother's stuff from her childhood was up in the attic, and a lot from generations before that. Mother and Papa had died together last Labor Day weekend. That was a bad shock, of course, but not the only one.

Andrew Carnegie said that if you die rich, you die disgraced. Well, Mother will be safe with Andrew, if they meet in heaven. She'd been living beyond her means for years. Way beyond.

Bobby Applegate One of the first things my future mother-in-law told me when we met was that *her* grandmother used to cross the street to avoid shaking hands with a man who was known to be Spending Principal. Those robber barons, who made their money before the income tax, you'd have thought their shit didn't smell. Oh, sorry.

Anyway, I was stunned at how little would be left, after Uncle Sam took his whack. Sydney Brant Moss, the Princess of Cleveland, Ohio, had not been one you could talk to about estate planning. The laws of mortality had been suspended in her case. That was her position and she stuck to it.

Eleanor Applegate Poor Mother. Being Lady Bountiful was her whole identity. After I got over the surprise, it made sense to me.

Bobby Applegate She did give a lot away, and got a lot of social mileage out of doing it. She also paid no attention at all to what her money guys were doing, even when she still had her marbles. Après elle, le déluge.

Sydney and Laurus Moss, late parents of this tribe, died exactly the way they wanted to, by the way. Together. In old age, on the last night of their last summer in a place they loved. A faulty heater was involved, but so was will. It was hard on the children, though, I admit that.

Sydney's mind had begun departing in wisps and then chunks years earlier, leaving her soul, that bright nightgown, to cope alone. This made her a much simpler being than she had been for most of her life. More like us. Laurus had had strokes and knew there would be more. He dreaded what would have come next for them: he unable to look after them both, and she long since unable to do much of anything except be grateful. (Not that that should be underestimated as a contribution to the common weal.)

Laurus appeared here almost immediately, and moved on just as quickly. Sydney, so far, is still elsewhere.

❧

Eleanor Applegate I'd been the one to do most of the cleanout of the house, and to deal with the officer at the bank and the lawyer who'd drawn up our parents' wills. They're both about a thousand years old and we think the lawyer has Alzheimer's. Monica had her hands full at home, and Jimmy lives in California . . . well, it fell to me.

The bank had all the stuff in the house appraised, for estate taxes, and I'd hired an auction woman to come in after us and sell what we didn't want. My daughter Nora had dreams of selling it all herself on eBay but we said no. I can't say she took it well. She graduates from college next month and hasn't a clue what comes next, and she saw this as about a year's employment. And I sympathize. I was already married when I graduated from college, but I know what that panic felt like.

So Monica and Jimmy and I were in the dining room with our lists of stuff we wanted. Charlesie, my youngest, came in and took a picture of us with an ancient Brownie box camera he found in the powder room. There was black-and-white film in it, and the picture actually came out afterward. We're standing in front of the sideboard armed with our pencils, with me in the middle in my Princess Di flip. I think I'm getting a little old for that hairdo. Monica is in blue jeans with her mad hair, which she won't color, on top of her head. I dislike noting that she's thinner than I am, which she never used to be. Also taller. Am I shrinking already? Jimmy has our father's face and build. His forehead is higher than when he was young but otherwise he's aging disgustingly well.

Monica Faithful Mother's will ordered that only the three of us could be in the room for the lottery, no spouses or children. Her motives weren't pure. She really never liked her grandchildren and she wasn't too sure about Josslyn. We'd have rather had everybody in on it, at least I would have, but we didn't know if Gradgrind from the bank might suddenly appear, lurking in the azaleas outside the windows, to make sure we were obeying Mother's cold dead hand reaching from the grave.

Although cold doesn't mean to us what it does to you. We are one with the weather. Such a pleasure, not to be plagued by one's senses. Now and then one has a fleeting memory—of scent, let us say. Not of lemon or lilac, but of what a scent was. One doesn't miss having it—that would be Hell, which is a very different matter. But to remember, for its own sake.

No, we haven't all lived, in the sense you mean. I have, once or twice, but was never very good at it. As here, I preferred to observe.

My last time, I took a stab at marriage, to a widow named Candace Brant, and acquired a family. This one, and I liked it more than I would have guessed. Now I can't quite break the habit of watching over them. Not to interfere, though of course we can. Just to see how they grow.

Monica Faithful By Lottery Weekend, the house was like a warehouse. Eleanor had been working all winter, hauling stained linens and partial sets of china and crystal down from the attic and up from the basement. Jimmy's kids were parading around the house in Mother's mink stoles (she had two of them. Why?) and Papa's concert clothes. The older girls ate dinner wearing Mother's New Look dresses from right after World War II, with the great big flouncy skirts. The dresses had matching hats, with veils. Mother used to erupt when the kids explored in the cedar closet, so now they all had to get into everything, if only to prove she wasn't coming back.

I had come to help Eleanor for one long weekend, and Eleanor's girls, Annie and Nora, had been there a lot. My stepdaughter Sylvie helped too. The chatter is wonderful when those three are together. Charlesie came once to do the grunt work, carrying broken juicers and ironing boards out to the Dumpster. When something broke, Mother didn't throw it out, she put it in a closet and bought another one. I found *two* dead Hoovers in the closet in my bedroom. My clothes from boarding school, pleated skirts, knee socks that I'd carefully put in mothballs, were all gone. Thrown out or given away or stolen by the drunk maid whose other trick was to show her tits in the back room at Hanratty's Grill downtown for a dime. But do we throw out dead vacuum cleaners? What if 1948 came back and they started working?

Bobby Applegate When the lottery began, the outlaws went into the sunroom. Josslyn was playing Monopoly with her children. She wears her hair down to her butt and she uses it like a shawl, or a curtain, or like something from the Dance of the Seven Veils. I couldn't tell how she could see, half the time. Anyway Jimmy's children are acquisitive little beezers; Virgil had two hotels on Boardwalk in about the first five minutes. Jimmy's children are named after cultural heroes. Jimmy got to name the firstborn. Josslyn named the next one. Regis.

Norman Faithful was showing me a present he bought Monica when they stopped in New York on the way to Connecticut. Why, I don't know. It was a little box made of silvery mesh. "So I got out the door and was walking toward Fifth Avenue when a guard from the museum taps me on the shoulder," Norman says, acting this all out. "The guard says, 'Excuse me, sir, but that box is not free.' I said, 'It certainly wasn't, it was bloody expensive.'" He had put it in his tote bag, hadn't let them put it in a store bag. He carries a canvas tote bag everywhere. "Nicky's a fanatic about refusing plastic bags," he says. The guard wants to see his receipt. Meanwhile half of New York has stopped to watch this drama.

(Monica is sometimes called Nika, NEEK-a, by people who have known her since childhood. Only her husband calls her Nicky. It's a little controlling to rename a person, isn't it? Of course, the kids call *him* Normal, but not to his face.)

I ask him if he was wearing his dog collar. Kind of loving the image of this great tall stringbean priest in the hands of the gendarmes.

"I was." Norman is meanwhile miming a desperate search of his pockets. "Finally I found the damn receipt in my wallet. Our audience was crushed not to see me wrestled to the ground and handcuffed."

"Did the guard offer to kiss your feet?"

"And back out of my presence? No. But he did apologize."

"You should have threatened to sue," says Josslyn from behind her hair.

After a silence, Norman says, "He was just trying to do his job."

Eleanor Moss Applegate We were determined not to be one of those families that comes unglued over who gets the special tea cozy. I thought we all worried more about getting crosswise with each other, as we got ready to divide the spoils, than about getting any particular treasure. But on the day, Monica was like spit on a griddle, as Ellen Gott used to say.

The Lottery According to Mother was to go like this. First we drew straws to see what order we would choose in, and it worked out Monica first, then me, then Jimmy. Then it reversed. With her first choice, Monica took a diamond brooch that belonged to Great-grandmother Annabelle.

It was almost the only good jewelry left, but I was surprised she took it. It's old-fashioned, in the shape of ribbons tied in a sparkly bow. She has nowhere to wear such a thing, and if she breaks it up, it's just a handful of not especially good diamonds. Nothing of which you could say, "This came to me from my mother."

I could have worn it.

Monica Faithful I don't know why I took the brooch. I surprised myself. Being in that house, picturing Mother going out in the evenings, I remembered being little and thinking that someday I'd be grown up and have diamonds too.

Now I'm fifty-three, and Eleanor wears big diamond studs in her ears for everyday, and I wear the same little gold hoops I bought when I had my ears pierced.

Eleanor Applegate I took Mother's writing desk from the living room. It was one of the few really valuable things in the house, but I wanted it because I could see her sitting at it in the mornings, paying her bills. Jimmy took the massive butler's desk from the old Elms, that Papa had used as a dresser. It will look ridiculous in his pastel house in California but we all knew he wanted it and were pleased that he got it.

Then it was Jimmy's turn again, since we chose in reverse order for the second round. I assumed he would take one of the sets of silverware. There are two: the Victorian set Mother used, and the Art Deco service our mother's mother, Candace, bought when she married Bernard. Mother raised us to despise our grandmother, but now that we were finally demobbed from our duties as foot soldiers in her many battles, we all found the Art Deco set much prettier.

But instead, Jimmy said, "I'll take Nina's piano." Monica looked absolutely stricken. Clearly she hadn't seen this as a possibility or she'd never have taken that pin.

"Why?" asks Monica in this flat voice.

"Josslyn wants Boedie to take lessons," says Jimmy, apparently puzzled. Did he *not* know?

Boedicia is their youngest. Jimmy refused to have a fourth child because Josslyn would have named it Jewel.

Monica Faithful, e-mail to Jeannie Israel The point was . . . why *this* piano? Why not buy some Yamaha spinet? Some damn thing Josslyn can paint sea-foam green? If she paints Aunt Nina's piano, or decoupages it or something, I'll have to kill her. Really.

Eleanor Applegate I didn't know what to do. So I said, "I'll take Mother's silver."

"I thought you wanted the other set," Jimmy says. He was right, but I couldn't stand the look on Monica's face.

Monica Faithful, e-mail to Jeannie Israel El said, "I can use the bigger set," and it's true, there is more of it, although a lot of it is Victorian weirdness, like marrow spoons or oyster forks. They can afford to entertain well, and they do.

Eleanor Applegate Monica can't entertain in a fancy way, and Norman wouldn't let her even if money weren't an issue. It is Monica's job, one of her very many unpaid jobs as rector's wife, to do nothing that would make her parishioners uncomfortable, like appearing rich or poor. Bobby says her job description appears to be "Wear Beige and Shut Up." But that doesn't mean she shouldn't have any nice things. Norman does, by the way. He's got a very spiffy Rolex Oyster watch, I notice.

Monica Faithful, e-mail to Jeannie Israel So I took the Art Deco silver. Then I had TWO things I couldn't use and didn't want. I might have taken it to sell, but now I can't even do that, since Eleanor left the one she wanted for me.

Eleanor Applegate Why would Josslyn want that piano? She never even *knew* Aunt Nina.

Everyone needs to be somebody's favorite. Monica was

Nina's. When Nina came to visit, rare as that was, since Mother couldn't bear her, she would play the piano for hours while Monica sat on the bench beside her and sang in her little piping voice. They went right through the *Fireside Book of American Folk Songs*; Aunt Nina could play anything at sight, and Monica loves to sing. Too bad she didn't get Mother's voice. Fortunately Norman's ear is worse than Monica's, so he doesn't notice that she's probably only welcome in the choir loft because she's the rector's wife. Well, also because they like her.

Monica Faithful, e-mail to Jeannie Israel So the next time it was my turn, I asked if I had to burn one of my turns to take Papa's car. It was a total foregone conclusion that it was mine. Norman and I had bought one-way airline tickets because we were going to drive it home. But Jimmy says, "Of course," as if this was all too amusing. "I was thinking we could keep it in Dundee to teach the kids to drive in. It gets better mileage than a Hummer..."

Eleanor Applegate What was he thinking? *Was* he thinking? It just was *not* the moment for teasing.

Monica Faithful, e-mail to Jeannie Israel So I said, "FINE, I take Papa's car," and then I had three things I didn't want. It's Norman who wants the Volvo. Then Ellie said, "I'll take the *Rolling Stone*." Papa's sailboat. And I lost it.

Jeannie Israel They're so polite with each other most of the time, you might not know how important these three are to each other. But with the parents dead and everything in the system shifting, they were beginning to sense that things could break that never had before. And none of them knew how their connections worked, so if they broke, how would they fix them?

You'd have had to see their mother playing them off against each other to understand how they learned to communicate by gesture, by indirection. If Sydney saw an alliance forming she'd attack; she loved a good game of "Let's You and Him Fight."

Growing up together makes you *familiar*, but that's a different thing from understanding each other.

Eleanor Applegate Monica said, "*What?* I didn't think we were doing Maine things until summer!" in this voice that didn't sound like her at all. I was totally confused. I said, "Did you *want* it?" Keeping a boat is expensive and Norman hates sailing.

She got up and ran out of the room. Jimmy and I were just looking at each other. Here we were with our pads, our pencils, and our lists.

We've seen enough of Mother rushing from the table in storms of tears to last a lifetime. If Monica's going to start turning into Sydney, I don't think I can take it.

Finally Jimmy said to me, "Well, do you have any idea why she married Norman in the first place?"

And what did *that* have to do with the price of eggs?

❧

Moral stages. We're unclear who invented them. It's amazing how much less we care here about things like who gets credit. Anyway, so useful. Stage one is infantile. I'm the center of the universe and everything flows to me or from me. Stage two: you scratch my back, I'll scratch yours. Or, I'll be good if I can see what's in it for me. Stage three: the group. I travel in a tribe, I want to fit in, I'll go along with what the group thinks is right. Stage four: Pharisees, Sadducees, and lawyers. The hegemony of the Rule Book. I am saved because I follow the rules, and if you don't, you're not. Stage five: outside the box. Stage fives think for themselves and you can't tell what they're going to do. Saints, suicides, Hitler, the Buddha, and Jesus Christ are all stage five, unless they're insane. Behaving without thinking doesn't count as a moral stage, or else it's stage one. Hard to explain perhaps, but to us it seems simple.

***

Jeannie Israel Very tall men live longer. They run companies and countries out of all proportion to how many there are of them. A very tall man makes you feel safe, because unconsciously you remember a time in your life when people taller than you had to make all the hard decisions. I had a boyfriend once who was six feet five. He was very shy and always wondered why people looked to him when there was confusion or people needed a decision. Then he met a guy who was six seven and he said he suddenly understood.

Kim Colwin I started dating Monica Moss when we were juniors in college. She was at Sarah Lawrence and I was at Princeton. Looking back, I think it was a little too easy for her. Our parents liked each other. The sociology was right. We looked great together. It was wonderful, like being in a bath that's exactly the right temperature. I thought, What's not to like about this? Slam dunk, you know?

Jeannie Israel In college Nika and I didn't see each other as much, but we wrote a lot, and saw each other every summer. I was very involved with campus politics, SNCC and SDS, and all that kind of washed right over Monica. I guess she had her own war going on the home front. But I thought Kim was great for her. He was maybe a little conventional, plus Monica's parents liked him and Kim's parents liked her. Nineteen sixty-nine wasn't really the year for young people doing what their parents hoped they would. Monica's sister Eleanor had eloped instead of letting Big Syd plan a fancy wedding for her. Jimmy, when he was home, had dirty hair down to his shoulders and was usually facedown in his soup plate, stoned to the gills, as Big Syd cooed and burbled about him. Monica's style in those days was mostly black leotards, shiny clean hair, no makeup. My father once said to her that she looked like a Jules Feiffer cartoon, and she did *not* think it was funny. I don't guess I would have either; we all felt very original. Monica's hair was long and straight, which I envied. I had to iron mine. This all drove Sydney crazy. She thought if her daughters didn't go to the hair parlor once a week like her and have permanents they were just wrong wrong wrong and people would talk behind her back about *her*. Sometimes Sydney would stop us at the door and forcibly paint her own lipstick on Monica. I don't know how Monica stood it; but she'd stand there quietly, and when we were outside the door, she scraped it off.

I'll never forget that actually, what it was like to have Mrs. Moss bearing down on us, holding the uncapped red lipstick like a weapon. To this day I can't wear Elizabeth Arden. It felt like assault, it really did.

Leonard Rashbaum I first met Monica and Kim at Harvard Law School. Monica was taking an ed degree. She wanted to teach first grade. To teach people to read. She *loved* reading. One winter weekend right before our first exams, which was a really terrifying time for One Ls, Monica came and sat in the library with us. While we studied, she read Dickens. I think she read three novels in one weekend, two thousand pages or something. She sat with her chin in her hand and didn't move except to turn pages. I'd never seen anything like it.

Kim was a really nice guy. Maybe not the sharpest knife in the drawer, but kind. Which you didn't get a lot of at the law school in those days. Monica was living on Garden Street, in a rented room in some lady's house, so she spent a lot of time with us. She'd bring her books over and study with us in the evenings at Langdell Hall. We'd go for coffee and talk about saving the world.

We were all going to open storefront offices in Harlem or the East Village and rescue the downtrodden; that was how we justified taking elite degrees while denouncing elitism. Of course when the time came, the job offers from Davis Polk and Milbank Tweed were just so rich and flattering, we began to say maybe we could do more good by changing the power structure from within. But that's another story.

Kim Colwin One evening in October, Monica came into the reading room really upset. She'd been wandering alone in the law school quad, thinking her thoughts, enjoying the smell of fall, the way you do, and when she came into Langdell she let the door drop closed behind her. We were all still at the stage of being kind of knocked out to be in that building where so many brilliant men had taught and learned. So there she was in the marble halls, minding her own business, thinking about Justice Frankfurter or something, when this voice behind her booms, "That was *incredibly* rude!" It was some guy she'd never seen before, in the usual law school mufti, blue jeans, a tweed jacket, wire-rimmed glasses. *Glaring* at her. She was shocked.

He said, "You knew I was behind you!" But she hadn't, she'd had no idea. He said, "Of course you did. You deliberately dropped the door in my face. Where were you raised, in a barn?"

Then he stomped off and Monica ran up to find us. She was undone.

Leonard Rashbaum I wanted to know who he was. She kept saying, "I had no idea he was there!" as if we might doubt her. She'd never even seen him before. I pointed out that *he* knew *her* perfectly well, even if he didn't know her name. Every guy who studied at Langdell knew the girls at least by sight. There weren't very many of them. I said, "He's probably in love with you."

We told her to tell us when she saw him again so we could tell him he was an asshole.

Kim Colwin She was always watching for him after that whenever she came to study with us, keeping an eye out for the Manners Police. It was as if a total stranger had said to her, "You have no idea who you are. *I* know who you are, and the news is not good." I'd never seen that side of her before. Why did she care?

Finally, at Harkness one evening we were having coffee when she leaned across to us and said, "There he is."

I said, "Who?"

She said, "The 'Raised in a Barn' guy. The tall guy at the cash register."

By the end of the week we knew his name was Norman Faithful, that he was a Two L, that he was married with children. He was supposed to be very smart on his feet, a hot litigator, but he lived off campus and no one seemed to know more about him than that. A cat who walked by himself.

Jeannie Israel As I understand it, Monica was out in the sun one afternoon in the spring, waiting for Kim, when she saw Norman Faithful coming toward her. He always looked as if he'd gotten some special map of the universe at birth, that everyone else had to put together piecemeal. Once she knew who he was, she had seen him fairly often. They always pretended not to see each other. This time he walked right up to her. He said, "Excuse me. I think I owe you an apology."

Instead of thinking, I'll say you do, asshole, she said she felt this wave of gratitude. He said, "Do you know what I'm talking about?"

And she thought that seemed like a reasonable question. He hadn't raped her or stabbed her or run over her dog. He'd spoken harshly to her when she didn't deserve it. It had probably never had anything to do with her. She figured she *might* have forgotten all about it, especially if she hadn't already been trained from childhood to expect to be suddenly found guilty and bad at the most random moments.

So she said then she noticed he had these very beautiful eyes, like shards of blue and green glass.

Kim Colwin They were sitting together over coffee in the Harkness cafeteria when I found them. Norman unfolded from the chair and towered over me. He introduced himself. I was seriously surprised. He said, "Join us?"

I didn't really think it was up to him to issue the invitation. I said I already had a caffeine headache, and he said, "Contracts exam coming up?" Which was kind of obvious, since I was holding the textbook and five pounds of notes. I said yes, and Norman said, "Good luck. You'll need it." Very pleasantly. I waited a minute to see if Monica would come with me but she didn't move. So I left.

Good luck—you'll need it? What kind of thing is that to say?

Eleanor Applegate I think the first thing I learned about Norman was that he had been a child prodigy, like Jimmy. It interested Monica a lot. Monica had asked about his name, since she'd never heard of anyone named Faithful except that English singer who slept with Mick Jagger. It's a made-up name. His father was an evangelical preacher in the Midwest somewhere. Little Norman had the gift too. He was calling people to repent when he was six; he could make grown men weep and open their wallets.

Of course Jimmy could do the same thing at the piano. Jimmy could hear a piece of music and play it back by ear when he was way too small to reach the pedals with his feet. Papa wanted him to slow down, learn to read, learn to play with understanding before he played in public, but Mother couldn't help herself—she loved an audience and this was sort of a Munchausen prodigy by proxy situation.

Monica Faithful Jimmy was such a gorgeous little boy. I think he actually liked it for a while. I guess anyone would like the applause and stuff, and he probably liked being taken out of school. He looked very cute in his little gray flannel jacket and shorts and his little bow tie. But one day he was supposed to go into New York with Mother to play at some fund-raiser, and he just refused to come out of his room. That was the end of it.

Eleanor Applegate Just wouldn't open the door until Mother left the house. Of course that wasn't the end of it ... Mother tried a couple of more times, and she wanted Papa to make him do it, but Papa wouldn't. He thought the whole thing was weird, like grinding a hurdy-gurdy. I'd have given an arm and leg to have Jimmy's gift. Would things have worked out differently if he'd been allowed to grow into it? To feel it was something that belonged to him, instead of to his mother?

So Norman had been like Jimmy. He had had this astounding ability in early childhood. He gave sermons, he did healings, then one day he refused to do it any more. Monica thought it was such an amazing coincidence, I sometimes wondered if it was true. Maybe Norman's gift isn't that he was a child prodigy; maybe it is that uncanny ability he has to sense exactly where the crack in your head is, and use it.

Jeannie Israel I never heard Jimmy play a note. He had already quit by the time we started going to Dundee in the summers and Nika and I fell in with each other. I asked him once what it was like for him to listen to music, to be around musicians. He spent some time in his twenties as a roadie for a band called Raging Biscuits or something. He said it was like listening to a language he used to speak but couldn't remember.

Monica Faithful The first thing that seemed to interest Norman about me was Jimmy. He wanted to meet him. I was about two-thirds fed up with Jimmy at the time, but I did see him now and then. He'd been up to Dundee the summer before, after Mama and Papa had left. He'd come out sailing with El and Bobby and me, and when we brought the boat in after a long day, and everyone was struggling to furl wet sails and clean out the galley, Jimmy stood on the deckhouse doing yoga with his eyes closed, as if he were just a child of God and couldn't be expected to do grunt work when the sunset was beautiful. Calling Harold Skimpole. I didn't think Norman and Jimmy were going to have a lot to talk about.

Leonard Rashbaum I'd always had a sneaker for Monica. One day in the spring of 1971, I ran into her on the T. I remember it was stinking hot and I was wearing a suit, coming from a job interview. Monica was the only person on the train who didn't look like she was melting. She had that pretty dark hair all on top of her head, and a barrette thing made of a piece of leather with a stick through it. She said she was student-teaching. She said she loved it. And she said she was getting married.

I said, "That's great, anyone I know?" I'd been thinking of going looking for her myself, but I don't know, I didn't think Kim was over her. I guess I waited too long.

She said, "Norman Faithful." I had a good laugh, then I looked at her face. I stopped and said, "Oh my god. You're not kidding."

Eleanor Applegate Maybe she *did* want the *Rolling Stone.* Oh dear. But Charlesie is the real sailor in the family. He spent the last two summers as Papa's boat boy, taking him out to the *Stone* every day to run the engine and pump the bilge, and talk him out of leaving the mooring. They'd get down in the engine compartment and look at things for hours. Charlesie loves that boat and he understands it. He can chart a course and do celestial navigation.

Edith Faithful I always thought Charlesie expected to get the boat, since he'd spent all that time keeping Grandpapa from going onto the rocks, or sailing off toward Spain, but it's not as if he did it for free. It was a job. I'd have loved to do it, but no one offered it to me.

Josslyn Moss Adam and Edith and I made lunch. *That* wasn't easy . . . it was Eleanor's kids who did the last grocery run and they bought cereal full of sugar and dyes, and whole fat milk, and supermarket cheese, already shredded. The only vinegar in the house you wouldn't douche with. I found an eggbeater with only one beater. The tea bags were Lipton. I wonder if Mr. and Mrs. Moss gassed themselves on purpose. *I would, if I ate like this.*

We opened cans of soup. We made toast, and a salad with iceberg lettuce. Nobody starved. We ate in the sunroom.

Jimmy didn't get any of the silver. He took the piano.

Why? I didn't show how disappointed I was. It's their stuff. I could buy some secondhand. But my mother never had silver and I liked that it was in the family.

Bobby Applegate Norman and I cleaned up after lunch, and he dropped the other shoe. I told Eleanor he would. I washed, he dried. We've learned, over the years, that if Norman washes he talks the whole time about what Saint Augustine meant or where Thomas à Becket's bones are really, and doesn't notice what he's doing and the next thing you know, you're taking clean plates out of the cupboard with strings of asparagus stuck to them. He said, "Can I ask you something? Did Eleanor show you her copy of the will?" I said, Of course. He said, "Nicky told me that when Jimmy was in his twenties, he asked for his share of the estate in advance. Is that true?"

I said it was.

"And they gave it to him?"

I said they did.

"Well then, why was the estate split three ways in the will?"

I said, "I was going to ask you. Don't you guys have a story about a prodigal son?"

At this point, I don't know where his towel is, but if these dishes are going to get dry they'll have to do it by themselves. He says, "We do, of course, but the Parables . . . well, you know there's almost no evidence that there was a historical figure called Jesus. No physical evidence, hardly any documentary evidence. Josephus mentions him, after the fact. There probably was a Jewish rabbi named Jesus put to death by Pontius Pilate, but the authentic Jesus, the only evidence we really have is his voice, you hear a voice in the Synoptic Gospels that no one could make up. I call him Jesus the Asshole."

I said I imagined that woke up the parishioners.

"No, not from the pulpit, of course not. But it's exciting, that voice." It was clearly exciting to Norman. He was revving up. "He says outrageous things. Like, Leave your parents and children. Give away all your money. The kingdom of heaven isn't fair, get over it."

"The prodigal son, Norman?" He's like a train running off track when he gets going.

"Yes. So, obviously, that parable is a classic example of Jesus the Asshole. It's an upsetting story. But you'll notice, the prodigal son is welcomed by his father. He is loved and celebrated and given honorable work. But it *doesn't* say he gets another share of the inheritance."

I said, they weren't my parents, it was never going to be my money, and I didn't think it was my business. But I got the impression that Norman thought it *was* going to be his money.

Carla Lowen I remember the time Monica first took Norman home to meet her parents. Not to Connecticut, she was taking him to Maine. It was August. They'd only been dating for a few months, but I knew it was serious, because she stayed in Cambridge most of that summer, even though she didn't have classes. She got a job doing research for some professor. Boston is beastly hot in the summer, and the house we lived in didn't have air conditioners. We had window fans. It was miserable.

Norman had left his wife and was living in Somerville.

He was a very compelling guy, very tall, thick hair, beautiful eyes. It was fun to listen to him talk, because he had a great memory and his mind worked fast. Though sometimes after he was gone you'd wonder, What was *that* all about? He had a summer job with some white-shoe law firm in Boston. Monica was excited that she and Norman were going to hitchhike to Maine. *That* would drive her parents crazy . . . My boyfriend had a little two-stroke motorcycle, an Indian, so I had a leather jacket. She borrowed that and wore blue jeans and she looked really cute, like an elegant teddy boy.

An hour later, she was back. Norman was furious at her. He expected her to know that she should go hitchhiking dressed as if she were going to tea with Mrs. Astor. She went out again in a sundress and heels, and Norman was right, they got a ride right away with a woman in a sports car who was going to Northeast Harbor. Norman sat in front and talked to the woman for five hours, and Monica sat stuffed in the tiny backseat with their duffel bags.

Amelia Crane Morriset Jeannie and I thought Norman was very attractive, that first summer we met him. He was charming, very disingenuous, if that's the word I want. So pleased with everything, so enthusiastic. Aunt Sydney fell over herself flirting with him. Maybe Sydney was trying to make a point to Eleanor, that she was really a lovely, easygoing mother-in-law. She'd never quite been able to get a handle on Bobby. And she'd been so upset when Bobby and Eleanor eloped, she wanted to be sure she wasn't going to get cut out of things again. She didn't need to worry, though. Norman had a way of knowing exactly how to talk to whoever was in charge of the honeypot.

Eleanor Applegate I don't think Mother and Papa learned about wife number one until about six weeks before the wedding. That wedding was huge, by the way. It was Monica's one big moment to be the most important person in the family, and she still wasn't. That wedding was all about me and Bobby, Mother showing off what we had missed. Monica wanted a morning wedding but it was in the evening because Sydney wanted a black-tie reception. Black tie! In Dundee, Maine, in August! No one even wears a dress suit to funerals in Dundee in August. A blazer and a tie without soup stains is as gussied up as we get.

Monica wanted the bridesmaids in simple linen sheaths we might be able to wear again but we ended up in these frothy floor-length numbers covered in eyelet. I was the matron of honor and still fat from my last pregnancy; I looked like a sno-cone. Norman asked Jimmy to be his best man, so right up to the moment she stood with Papa to walk down the aisle, Monica had to worry whether the best man would show up, or be able to *stand* up. I was amazed that Jimmy came at all, we hardly ever saw him in those years.

Annie was to be the flower girl, but Adam was too little to be ring bearer and Mother announced that she was going to rent one. Monica drew the line at that, even trying as hard as she could to have this perfect mother/daughter experience. Sydney couldn't understand it. She'd eloped, I'd eloped, this was her chance to have a picture-perfect wedding and Monica was standing in her way. "A cute little blond boy in a tiny blazer, with the ring sewn onto a little satin pillow," Sydney kept saying. Monica announced that the ring bearer would be Norman's son. It took a lot to stop Sydney in full spate, but that did it.

Amelia Crane Morriset Norman never talked about the first marriage. It was as if he'd ordered a dish he didn't like at a restaurant. He'd sent it back to the kitchen and ordered something else, end of story.

Eleanor Applegate Monica barely knew those children when she married Norman. She was very starry-eyed about them, but their mother didn't want them to have anything to do with Monica. She certainly wouldn't let them be in the wedding, but we did keep Mother from renting any more children for the bridal party.

Norman claimed that he woke up one morning and noticed that he had married the worst person in the world. He said she had a rage disorder. Her name was Rachel Cohen and she lives in Boston; I run into her from time to time. I was sympathetic to Norman; it's no fun to live with a person who might explode at any moment, said the voice of experience, Child of Sydney. Apparently once Rachel threw his suits into the bathtub and set them on fire so he wouldn't have anything to wear to work. *That's* not normal. But I begin to think there may well have been two sides to that story.

Bobby Applegate There are always two sides in a marriage. Always. At least two.

Norman Faithful I remember two things clearly from the summer of 1971. One was, I had to buy a tuxedo for my wedding. I'd never owned one. The other was that Nicky and I took her father's yacht out to Beal Island one day by ourselves. I usually get seasick, but that day I was golden. I had been out to the island the summer before, with Nicky's parents. We'd had a picnic at March Cove. I remember I had hitchhiked up from Boston the day before and I was still stiff from sitting in this woman's little sports car, way too small for a man my height, but it was a lucky break that she stopped for me, since she was going to Maine as well, even farther north than I was, and she brought me all the way into Dundee.

That was the first time I ever saw the place. I remember Nicky and Mrs. Moss on the porch of Leeway waiting for me, and the smell of pine and musty books when you stepped inside. The whole weekend is etched, I knew then that my life was changing.

Anyway this next summer, Nicky and I sailed to Beal by ourselves. She wanted to show me the old graveyard. There used to be a settlement out on the island, but these days, there are only hunting shacks. It's not so easy to find the graveyard, you have to know where it is.

It's a beautiful spot on the crest of the island with views to the south past the outer islands to the Atlantic. We had our lunch and then we walked north on what must once have been the main road between farms or settlements. A grassy path wide enough for a wagon. Then the most amazing thing happened. I heard someone weeping, right near us. I said, "Nicky, stop. What's that?" She couldn't hear it at all. It sounded to me like a woman. We'd walk on, then I'd hear it again. I'd stop, and look, and there was nothing but these heartbroken pleading sobs coming from just out of my field of vision. Very eerie.

We saw a meadow with a couple of apple trees, and a

clump of huge alders and other trees that Nicky said meant an old cellar hole was there. We decided to go exploring. The whole world had gone silent, except for that rustle and buzz that summer makes. We found the boulders that must have made up the foundation of a house or barn lining a pit that was filled now with a huge pine and some scrub. A little rusty-colored snake about a foot long was sunning itself on one of the boulders. Before I could show it to Monica, zip! It was gone. A small path led off toward the wood, and we decided to follow it. We'd gone only a few steps when Boom! there was this thunderous flapflapflapping right beside us. I nearly jumped out of my skin. Out of the meadow rose a blue heron. Gorgeous. A farm pond was concealed in the high grass there where she'd been taking the sun, and we must have scared her more than she scared us. She was utterly lovely.

I felt as if some sort of veil that separates us from God's creation had dropped for a moment, that the heron and the weeping woman were all one thing, but Nicky thought it was creepy, that I could hear something that she couldn't, so we went back to the boat.

I kept thinking about that out-of-body weeping. It made me think of Mary Magdalene, with her Lord dead in the tomb. Why could I hear it, and not Nicky? It seemed like a message from the universe. Okay, Norman. You've had your time in the desert. You've built your known world out of the rules of men. Now it's time to turn to what that world of laws leaves out, that still can't be explained or denied. I'd *heard* that heartbroken weeping from a woman who wasn't there. What was I going to do, decide I didn't believe it?

I mentioned it the next day down at the post office. In

Dundee they don't have RFD, everyone goes to the post office every morning. The postmaster said, "Nobody's heard from *her* in a long time. Did you see her?" I said I hadn't, but was intrigued that others knew about her. I knew I hadn't imagined it. I asked if he knew who she was. He said, "Some think they do. You must have gone up into the graveyard. That gets her going."

Isn't *that* interesting?

Bobby Applegate I assume they went out to the graveyard to screw. It's secluded and peaceful and you're not afraid your future mother-in-law is going to come popping in on you. Some of my fondest memories involve that graveyard. But we never heard anything weird out there.

Monica Faithful A lot of out-of-towners came to the wedding. Mother had all her Connecticut friends up. Jeannie was maid of honor, and Eleanor matron. Norman had some friends from law school. And of course, his mother. I had met Norman's mother once. We went out to Indiana for Thanksgiving to tell her we were getting married. She must have known that's what we'd come to tell her, but she didn't make it easy. There was a lot of sighing over Thanksgiving without children. She had pictures of the Happy Family all over the living room, Norman and Rachel with Sam and Sylvia.

I was determined to make Hazel love me. I was going to be the perfect daughter-in-law.

Jeannie Israel Mrs. Faithful was a tough nut. In my clinical opinion, she was in love with Norman. I sat beside her at the rehearsal dinner, which Monica's grandmother gave at her house since Norman's mother had no idea that usually the groom's family did that. It was lobster, to give the out-of-towners a treat. Mrs. Faithful had never eaten one, and she didn't know not to wear her Sunday best. She was mostly silent, struggling with this red armored bug on her plate. I showed her how to use the cracker to open the claws and she tried it and fish juice squirted all over her dress, which looked like her church dress to me. Silk, with a white shawl collar. Oh dear.

⁂

My wife and I gave that party. They called me Uncle Bernard. Eleanor was my special charge, but they were all fond of me. I think.

I was very good at giving parties and presents, because I watched well, and remembered.

⁂

Eleanor Applegate I looked across the table just as Norman's mother got lobster guts right down the front of her dress. Jeannie Courtemanche was trying to help her, but on the other side, right at that moment, Jimmy started to eat with his hands. Hazel went critical. Her face got this closed-up stony expression. She sat eating coleslaw with her fork, trying not to let it get involved with the fish juice while her lobster lay there draining on the plate. When the serving girl asked if she was still eating, she just shook her head with her lips pursed. Jimmy said, "I'll take it," and lifted it right off her plate and started to eat it with his fingers.

Bobby Applegate That was a bad scene. It was August, so the lobsters were shedders, and they're messy, they just are. Hazel's condition improved when they passed the wipes and you could clean your hands, but then the toasts began, and I guess she'd never seen anything like it. The Danish cousins tried very hard to be nice to her but Kjeld said she kept referring to Monica as "an heiress." She was good and sick of the whole lot of us by the time she left town.

Monica Faithful We got off to a bad start. None of us had realized in advance that it would be so foreign to Hazel and she'd take it personally. We meant so well. Except maybe Mother, but even she had worked hard, and tried to make it perfect for everybody. She was never going to be best friends with Bobby's parents and I truly think she'd meant to take Norman's mother up, to show her a great time, adopt her. She pictured them as pals, taking care of the grandkids to-gether, that sort of thing. Sorry, wrong number.

Norman Faithful I don't think Mama was feeling well at our wedding. She was quieter than usual. But she's never been a boisterous person and I'm sure she enjoyed it. Syd-ney was at her best and I was pleased that Mama got to see her do her stuff.

Eleanor Applegate Mother was at her worst, of course. Bobby's parents didn't come, which annoyed her no end. They sent a beautiful silver cream and sugar on a little ham-mered silver tray from Tiffany, and Sydney put it in a corner mostly hidden by a huge vase from the Maitlands. The pres-ents were all laid out at The Plywoods on tables draped in white cloths, with the gift cards from each person propped in front of the gifts. Except for the Applegates' cream and sugar. Somehow she misplaced the card for that one.

The Plywoods? Grandmother Candace's "cottage." She'd torn down the summerhouse Mother grew up in, which had stairs that were hard for Uncle Bernard and was impossible to heat, and built a big modern ranch house on the site. It was supposed to be called The Elms, after the old house, but Mother refused. When Candace died, Mother sold it practically before the will was read. She never even asked us how we felt about it.

Amelia Crane Morriset Norman gave the best toast I'd ever heard, bar none. He looked sensationally handsome and he spoke without notes. He thanked the Mosses for the parties and for welcoming him, and then he toasted his bride . . . standard stuff, I know, but it brought me to tears. For a split second, I was actually jealous of Monica.

Monica Faithful We moved into a parlor-floor apartment in Back Bay. I loved my job and Norman was doing well at Ropes & Gray. We took Norman's children every other weekend. At first they were like feral animals. Sam was four and the baby, Sylvie, was just over two. Sam used to hiss at me when I came into the room. Once he actually spat, but Norman had him out of his chair and over his knee for a whack on his bottom with scary speed. He said, "Don't you *ever* show disrespect to your stepmother again. Don't you ever show disrespect to any woman again, not even your sister." He was like an Old Testament prophet. After that, Sam only behaved that way when his father wasn't in the house. He was mad at me because I wouldn't let him put ginger ale on his cornflakes.

Jeannie Israel When I first met the children, I thought they were appalling. I was doing my psych Ph.D. at the time, so a little inclined to diagnose everybody, but really, they were ferocious little things. I thought the boy might be possessed. It happens.

Eleanor Applegate Monica was amazing. With your own kids you've got some instinctive connection. You're in love with them, they're part of you. Monica was without a road map with those two, but she was patient most of the time.

Bobby Applegate I thought they should have been drowned at birth, Norman's children. I offered to do it myself, but Monica discouraged it.

Monica Faithful I made a wonderful kid's bedroom out of the room Norman wanted to use for his study. I got bunk beds and made Marimekko curtains, and let the children each choose a color for one wall. Sam's wall was the color of eggplant; Sylvie's was orange. I did the painting myself and I brought them a little play desk from home. I brought a lot of my favorite books from my childhood and put them in their bookshelves. Then one day I came home from school and found Norman home from work hours early. I asked him what was the matter, but I could see he wasn't sick; if anything he was entirely too well. He was excited, sort of inflated, and he couldn't sit down; he was pacing up and down and gesturing with his arms, the way he does.

My first thought was that he'd been fired. But no. He

said, "Today Mr. Cantwell offered me a raise and a change of title. He said he was very impressed with my work and the partners wanted me on track to join them."

I said that was wonderful, because it was, it was much much sooner than we had any right to expect. I said, "Darling, how fantastic," or something like that and went to give him a kiss. In my head I was already thinking about what we'd do with the extra money. But Norman wasn't through. Mr. Cantwell invited him to lunch to celebrate, and Norman's answer was "No, thank you, I have thought about this for a long time and I've come to understand that Christ has a different plan for me." Then he resigned.

Jeannie Israel Monica called me and said she needed a break, and I asked her to come to New York for the weekend. She took the train down Saturday. I'd bought theater tickets, but we never went. She spent a lot of the time crying. She couldn't understand how a man with alimony, child support, and I don't know how many thousands in student loans to pay off could quit the best law firm in Boston to go to seminary. How was he going to pay for *that,* she kept asking.

She was frightened. She didn't have any money of her own. Her grandmother paid her tuition, but she didn't keep a car in college, or take fancy trips or spend money on clothes. She was afraid that Norman thought she could pay off his loans, or put him through seminary, or both. She was shocked at that.

I asked her if she believed in him and she said yes. I asked her if she believed he'd had a true call from God, and she said she guessed *he* believed it. We had both grown up in pretty secular households.

What kind of man does a thing like that without discussing it with his wife? Without even seeing that he *should* have discussed it with his wife?

Owen Cantwell Norman Faithful may have been the most talented litigator I ever saw. There's a quality you have to be born with. Jack Kennedy had it. When Norman was on his feet talking, you couldn't look away. And his memory was phenomenal. I was dumbfounded when he turned me down. He had his detractors in the firm, but the rising young Turks always do. I had put a lot of eggs in his basket, pushing him for partner track so early, and I came away with some of it on my face. I told him, you can survive doing this in public once, but don't make a habit of it. I was thinking that he meant to run for office down the line. I never pegged him for a priest. Never.

Bobby Applegate We had rented a tiny house up on the mountain that summer. On the Dump Road. The real estate lady called it "Turkey Farm Road," but I preferred Dump. I wanted to buy it so I could have Dump Road on my stationery. One night during their visit Norman and Monica came up to supper with us, and Norman announced that he had quit the law to become a priest. I was speechless. Eleanor blurted out, "Why?"

Eleanor Applegate He said he'd come to know Christ had a plan for him. I asked him *how* he'd come to know that. A voice spoke from clouds? Monica said that not all calls are so dramatic, and that she thought it was very exciting.

Ted Wineapple In our church there is quite a tough pro-cess, "discernment," it's called, where you have to get per-mission from the priest in your own parish, and a committee, and a lay mentor and the bishop in your diocese, to be a candidate for ordination. I had to go through an entire year of counseling and prayer and testing of various sorts before I could apply to seminary. The year before mine, our bishop hadn't recommended a single candidate to go forward. Nor-man managed to get the process speeded up in some way. I asked him about it years later and he just said, "That ave-nue's closed now."

Jimmy Moss I don't remember what I thought at the time about Norman's sudden conversion to Christianity. Saint Paul on the road to Damascus. I wish I did. I was pursuing various vision quests of my own in those years, and I'd have been interested, but what can I say.

Jeannie Israel I assumed he'd go to divinity school at Har-vard. Norman was really good at school, and let's face it, he likes the fancy brand names. But he chose General Theological. Maybe he had a contact there; the doors opened fast for him. I was only glad they'd be in New York. I only saw Nika briefly in the summers these years, and I missed her. All those summer days when we were kids, when whoever finished breakfast first turned up on the other one's porch, and we'd be off to meet Amelia in the lane, and then on foot, on bikes, or in little boats out into our day.

Monica Faithful What troubled me was leaving Sam and Sylvie. They were so young to have their father far away, and Rachel had full custody and certainly wasn't going to let them travel to us on weekends. But Norman was serenely confident. He knew what the Lord wanted him to do, and where, and he knew he had to get on with it. I'd like to think he was also trying to protect me—our marriage. I couldn't deny that the children strained things.

What I *did* like, very much, was that the whole curriculum of the marriage changed. Instead of talking about, I don't know, which senior partner wasn't pulling his weight and which brownnosing associate was getting all the good cases, suddenly we were all about Bible studies, and liturgy and church history. We started reading Compline aloud together every night, and it was so beautiful. So comforting, so mysterious. I began to have glimpses of ... I guess *wonder* is the word. That it might be possible to open an inner door to another world, to live in it or be filled with it. It was thrilling. Literally. Living with a person who is engaged with faith is a revelation.

❦

Of course you want to know what prayer is. Whether it works. Oh Lord, won't you buy me a Mercedes-Benz.

Of course it works. It works on the one who prays, like water pouring over rocks without being changed or broken, fitting through crevices, quietly turning fissures into ravines. And in turn it changes the universe, through the actions of those changed by praying. Praying, chanting, meditating, spirit dancing. Every culture has prayer forms, and words for them. For some natures the work is like hammering rocks, for some it's as simple as breathing, and for all it grows by itself with practice. Ask and it shall be given. Seek and ye shall find. Those are not tricks or riddles, but simple truths.

Unless you were serious about the Mercedes-Benz.

❦

Jeannie Israel They had a little apartment across the street from General. It's beautiful, General Theological Seminary, a peaceful cloister inside a brick wall in the midst of the city. Monica loved the chapel especially, but she also loved the whole conversation that went on. About the Bible. About Jesus. We'd both been dragged to Sunday school as children and Nika sang in the choir at boarding school because she liked singing. We'd heard a lot of Bible readings in our day, but did we understand them? Who the Gospels were addressed to, what the Old Testament had to do with the New Testament? No. Really shockingly little.

Monica loved learning things. That first year, they'd moved too late for her to get a teaching job, so she was subbing. She had time to listen to the seminarians, and to read Norman's texts on the lectionaries and things. We didn't talk about faith as such at the time, but I had the feeling that was because she felt she'd pitched forward into a tub of butter and it would be rude to go on about it to those who hadn't.

Monica Faithful Because we had moved to New York and didn't see the children during the school year, I got them for half of summer vacation. I remember being terrified of how Mother was going to react when Sam fed his lunch to the dog from the table, or stood on the cane-seat chairs with his cowboy boots on, but instead I found myself in a competition with her. She just loved Norman. He flirted with her and asked her advice. They even started praying together for a while. So of course she wanted Sam and Sylvie to think Leeway was the best place in the world and that she was the world's best grandmother. She was really pretty great that summer, except for the Affair of the Potion.

Ellen Gott I remember the summer Norman's children first came to the cottage for the month. I'll never forget it, I mean. *Please* and *thank you* were a foreign language. The little girl wet her bed so many times we had to throw the mattress out. Mrs. Moss was determined to love them to death, but when the boy made a "magic potion" out of Pepto-Bismol, her whole bottle of Chanel no. 5, and Mr. Moss's prescription pills, *that* was over. Monica couldn't eat, afraid of what her mother would do. I don't remember what happened next.

Eleanor Applegate That was the year that Jimmy asked to have his inheritance in advance, and my parents gave it to him. I mean, they *knew* he was going to piss it all away, they knew he was going to sniff it or smoke it or give it all to some cult, to see what it was like to have nothing but lice and a begging bowl. What were they thinking?

Bobby Applegate I wonder what the conversation was like, when Sydney and Laurus were deciding whether to do what Jimmy asked. Here is their firstborn, Eleanor, a model citizen in every way, a college graduate, married, a mother . . .

I had just gone to work for my brother and *we* could have used an infusion of capital, I promise you.

Eleanor Applegate It wasn't the money. I mean, it wasn't *not* the money, but what I minded was knowing that if *I* had asked, or Monica, we'd have been insulted or laughed at. Jimmy was just on a different plane for Mother. It didn't matter what I said or did, or how many As Monica got. Don't all those parables begin "The Kingdom of Heaven Is Like This"? Help.

The hardest part for most, when they first arrive here, is under-standing that they're dead. It's every bit as shocking as being born. (Being born! The lights, the noise, the air on your skin . . . I still shudder.) At first, some keep going back, sure there's been a mis-take, especially if the departure was abrupt. If they're angry or persistent enough they make themselves felt, even seen or heard. A few find this perversely thrilling and keep it up, beyond the nor-mal leavetaking or comforting of those left behind. Not a good choice. They can get stuck outside the great flow of spiritual mat-ter. But most soon find that the life they just lived in the body is less and less compelling. Perhaps like a long distance call on a signal that breaks up, so when it fades out altogether it comes as a relief.

Usually there will be guides waiting to help. Then new steps and stages. Just as you were taught, just as you expected. Masks and dodges forged in life fall away, and what remains is what you chose to become, with all those choices you made every day when in the body. It's very interesting. Free will.

Edith Faithful I'm named Edith Bing for my Danish great-grandmother, but I look like my father. Mother's eyes, but the rest of it. I'm six feet tall. As you can see I like that; I wear high heels. But inside I have Mother's brain. Neither of us can do math or read maps.

For the lottery, I was sharing the maid's room on the third floor with Sylvie. Sam was in California, and couldn't come, but we had his list.

At lunch, Mom told me she hadn't gotten Nina's piano for me. She was quite unwrapped about it. I'd love to have something of Nina's but I don't play any more, and they have a piano at the rectory. It belonged to my grandmother Hazel and it isn't very good but how much does that matter if it's never played? She got me a set of silver instead. Meanwhile, Sam wanted the monogrammed barware, and Sylvie wanted Granny Syd's fur coat, and I wanted the beautiful topaz ring Granny Syd wore when she dressed up. There's a story there.

Nora Applegate Annie and I were bunking in the bedroom above Grandpapa's music studio, and Adam and Charlesie slept downstairs on the couches. There's a TV and VCR, so at Christmas and such we tended to congregate there in the evenings while the 'rents played bridge in the house, or whatever they did.

Annie Applegate Uncle Jimmy's a scary-good bridge player. I played a lot in college, but he's way out of my league.

Mummy and Dad are both good. Normal is terrible because he never shuts up. Josslyn doesn't play. Aunt Monica only plays if they need her; she'd rather read. And let's face it, the last year or two, she's been pretty deep into the chardonnay in the evenings. Daddy plays just the same, sober or plastered (ask me how I know), but most people don't.

Nora Applegate After dinner the night before the lottery no one was even thinking of playing bridge or going to bed. Everyone started going from room to room again, opening drawers or pawing through boxes and saying, Oh my God, look at this. It was exhilarating. We were all still up at two or three in the morning. I found a picture of Mom and Monica dressed in matching Hopalong Cassidy outfits, with little cap guns in their holsters. Mom was a little chubby, and the hair was unfortunate. Monica had this cute little Dutch-boy haircut.

Jimmy Moss I walked into the playroom downstairs and found Monica sitting on the floor in her robe and jammies, wearing a mink cape and a church hat of Mother's, and long blue kid gloves. It had gotten cold down there so she put on whatever was at hand. She's a very droll woman, my sister. We sat down there for over an hour, sorting photographs. Astronomers must feel like this when they get a bigger telescope. Suddenly you can see past your own little galaxy, to the older worlds of astral matter you're made of. It was always *there*, you could sort of know that, but it's different to see it.

Monica Faithful We found a snapshot of Eleanor and Bobby on their wedding day in New York. El is wearing dark lipstick and a new spring suit and high heels, very pretty with her small waist and the big gazongas. I *remember* when that picture arrived at the house. Bobby's mother sent it. Bobby's father had been their witness and he was in the picture, and Mother had actually taken a pair of scissors and cut off that side of the picture!

Nora Applegate The only person who didn't seem to be into it was Uncle Norman. I went up to the attic, to look in the maids' rooms' closets and under the beds, since Granny Syd had stashed things everywhere, and there was Normal, pacing up and down the hall with his cell phone to his ear. He was listening to someone. He looked startled to see me, and said something like, "Yes, I'm here, go on..." and I waved at him and beetled off to the cedar closet. There were still some boxes up on the shelves that hadn't been gone through. I found someone's wedding dress, like from a museum, with little seed pearls sewn on, and a train and everything. I ran to get Mummy.

Eleanor Applegate We rushed upstairs. Norman was up there on his cell phone in the hall, oblivious. Nora had found Great-grandmother Annabelle's wedding dress. I thought at first it was Candace's but there's a picture of James and Candace on their wedding day, and she was wearing satin, with no lace or train. And besides, would Mother have kept the dread Candace's wedding dress if she'd ever had it? This was more froufrou and much older, we thought. The bodice was tiny, too small for Monica or me at any time in our lives, let alone now, but Nora is a sylph. We got her into it.

Monica Faithful I do think Mother would have kept Candace's wedding dress if she'd had it. I think that was always a love-hate thing for her, that she went on hoping until the end of Candace's life for some sign that her mother actually loved her. But Candace actually didn't. Sydney just wasn't her type. Poor Mother. But Nora in Great-grandmother's wedding dress! Ooh-lala! The sleeves were ivory lace and the veil fastened on with combs, which of course wouldn't work unless you have long hair pinned up to stick the combs into. We had to improvise. There were about a hundred little pearl buttons that had to be done up in the back. Even the matching shoes were there but those were much too small. Ellie and I hummed "Here Comes the Bride" and carried the train as Nora made her way down the stairs, to show everyone.

Eleanor Applegate And as we went by, Norman was still on the phone!

Sylvia Faithful You should know, by the way, that the most striking thing about this story is that my father was *listening* to somebody.

Josslyn Moss I was in the dining room putting numbers on things for the lottery when Nora came down in the wedding dress. I *ran* to get Boedie out of bed. Boedie said, "Nora looks just like Beauty in *Beauty and the Beast!*"

Eleanor Applegate We did get the lottery going again. Monica came back into the dining room, and before she could speak, I said I thought she was right, we should save Maine things for the summer. And she said, no no, we should decide about the *Rolling Stone*, soon it would be time for someone to pay the yard bills. I said, well, Charlesie sort of wanted to take care of the boat himself. He loves to work with his hands. And he really knows that boat, and we thought it would be good for him, to have something of his own to take care of. Monica said, "A wooden boat? How could he do all that himself, with the brightwork and so forth?" Of course, a wooden boat *is* a lot of work.

Monica Faithful My idea was that maybe Sam and Charlesie could own the boat together. I thought it would be a bonding thing. And I worried about Charlesie letting the boat go to seed; I'd rather see it sold out of the family than that. It took Charlesie a week flat driving Daddy's beloved old Nashcan before he'd broken an axle hot-rodding down the French Camp Road.

Eleanor Applegate The situation was a little tense. I know Monica hadn't forgotten the time Papa gave Charlesie his Nash. Not that the car was worth anything at that point; you could total it by losing the key. But I don't think she realized that that was years ago, Charlesie has grown up a lot. And I don't believe Edie cares about the boat. If Monica wants it for Sam and Sylvie—well, they're not Papa's blood. You know? It doesn't seem exactly right to me.

Jimmy Moss They were trying so hard not to say offensive things out loud about each other's children that I thought we might sit there staring at each other all afternoon. So I said, "Why doesn't Charlesie take care of the starboard side and Monica's children take the port side?" Nobody laughed. Then Eleanor said, "All right. I'll take the chandelier." We all looked up at it and I could imagine Josslyn swearing because she hadn't put the chandelier on her list.

Nora Applegate I became the family archivist. Mother said she'd pay me to set up a system and sort all the mystery photographs, the old letters (there were trunkfuls in the attic), the scrapbooks, all that. Charlesie and I spent the afternoon of the lottery in the playroom; he was taking photographs of great-great-uncle so-and-so out of crumbly old frames nobody wanted. Aunt Josslyn was with us for a while. She came up with a picture of a family on a porch in what looked like Maine. Summer, anyway. I didn't recognize anybody. Granny Syd would have known in a minute all about it . . . there was so much I wish we'd asked her when we could have.

In this picture there's a man with big mustaches standing with a violin in his hand, his wife (I'm guessing) sitting in front of him and a girl of about eighteen and a boy who's maybe ten. They're all in their Sunday best and looking grim, the way they do in old pictures where they had to hold still a really long time. It was Josslyn who noticed that the mother is wearing Granny Syd's topaz ring. But who were they? Why do we have their picture?

Eleanor Applegate Of course, in retrospect I understand why Monica was such a mess that weekend. I don't know how much she knew about Norman at the time, but certainly she knew something. Even if she didn't know she knew. We did get through the lottery afternoon, but there was still one big elephant in the living room. What were we going to do about the summerhouse? Bobby and I have our own house in Dundee. If it were up to us, we'd sell Leeway Cottage and use our share of the money to build a guesthouse, for when our children get married and have children of their own. But selling Leeway would leave Monica no place in Dundee, and it's important to all of us that we're all three there. Meanwhile Josslyn's started referring to Leeway as "the family homestead." Her way of saying it's her children's mess of potage more than Monica's stepchildren's. And probably that she'd like it all for herself, if she had her druthers.

Monica Faithful I was terrified Eleanor would force the issue. But Jimmy came to the rescue. He said, "Let's just try to share Leeway this summer as if Mother and Papa were still alive. It's big enough. If it doesn't work, we'll rethink it after Labor Day."

Bobby Applegate A recipe for total disaster if you ask me. But nobody did.

Edith Faithful I got the topaz ring. But Annie got the mink coat that Sylvie wanted. It was the only thing Sylvie really did want. She'd never buy new fur, but she gets cold in New York in winter. I felt bad for her. Mother had to choose between taking the coat for her or the ring for me.

Meanwhile Nora found rooms in the cellar we hadn't even known were there. In the furnace room she found a crate with business records from the 1880s, which I guess will explain where the Brant money came from. Now that it's mostly gone. She found a couple of trunks that belonged to Granny Candace's strange mountain-man brother, who has a peak in the Rockies named for him. And Annabelle Brant's Line a Days, and her scrapbooks. And then across from the furnace room, she found a bomb shelter.

Bobby Applegate Nora came running to get me. She had the ring of keys from the kitchen, and had opened a door I'd never even noticed. What was in there must have been some good idea from the fifties. There were big glass jugs of water, turned quite a nasty color, and a gallon of Scotch, and a carton of Kent cigarettes. A shelf of canned goods, some folded cots, and a card table and folding chairs. A transistor radio, all corroded. A first-aid kit. A couple of decks of cards and a set of dominoes. Can you imagine?

Eleanor Applegate And what were we supposed to do with fifty-year-old canned goods? We're always prepared for the wrong disaster.

Bobby Applegate I kept the Scotch.

Annie Applegate I spent an hour or two with the scrapbooks Annabelle Brant had made. Nora was trying to sort the family pictures in some way that made sense, the Mosses and Bings in their boxes and the Brants and Lees in others. We got pretty good at spotting great-aunts and -uncles, even in childhood. James Brant was easy; he was amazingly handsome, with a square jaw, and thick dark hair with a curl at the peak. There was a big picture of him in a silver frame on the piano, and also an oil of him and his sister

Louisa, who was retarded or demented or something, when they were about eight and ten. Uncle Jimmy took the painting, which surprised Mom, who had a place all picked out for it.

Annabelle's scrapbook had all the clippings about her wedding in Cleveland, and pictures of people we can't identify and lots of memorabilia from when James and Poor Auntie Louisa were small. Certificates of merit from Sunday school, invitations to parties. Pictures of The Elms in Dundee, not The Plywoods but the original house, when it was new. Pictures of Annabelle and James on some enormous yacht with the crew all in uniforms—I think it was the Maitlands'. Programs from concerts eighty years ago at Ischl Hall. Then a picture of James with a woman I didn't recognize. They're sitting under a tree in summer. Nora went burrowing through the laundry basket of pictures she either hadn't sorted yet or didn't know what to do with.

Nora Applegate Bingo—the woman with James Brant was the girl from the mystery family on a porch in Maine. The mother in that picture is wearing the topaz ring.

Annie Applegate Daddy said our great-grandfather was married before he married the Dreaded Candace. (And no one ever told us this?) The first wife's name was Berthe Hanenburger and the family were famous musicians who went to Dundee in the summer. Berthe died young. And apparently we kept the ring. Later I found a scrapbook all about her singing career, with lots of pictures of her from Cleveland and New York newspapers but nothing about her death. Dad thinks that poor Berthe died because she laced her corsets too tight while she was pregnant. But Aunt Monica said she had TB and lost her voice and shot herself.

Once I understood where the ring came from, *I* wanted it. It's hard, dividing this stuff. It isn't really bits of stone and metal and wood. It's the history of our family. Who loved who, who was cruel, who was kind. When I look at the pictures of those children, dressed up and hopeful, I think of all the things they must have longed for when they were young—puppies, a pony—and how long they've all been dead and buried, the children *and* the ponies. What's left is us.

Monica Faithful The woman who was doing the estate sale arrived as we were packing to leave the house for the last time. It was a beautiful morning. Those huge elm trees behind the house were in leaf, arching over the lawn. It was the trees that really got to me. We have parishioners up on the Heights in Sweetwater with trees like that, but the one big tree we had at the rectory was an ancient spruce that blew down in a storm last winter, right onto the roof of the garage.

I didn't want to linger any more, it was too complicated. I just wanted to pack the car and go.

Edith Faithful The auction lady wasn't very happy. She'd been planning to use the dining room to do her cataloguing. But at the last minute Uncle Jimmy took the dining room table, and of course Aunt Eleanor took the chandelier. The movers were taking it down as the lady walked in the door.

Dad was out in the driveway with the Volvo packed.

Standing there with the driver's door open. We'd have been ready to leave sooner if he'd come in and helped, but he had ants in his pants—he stood out there so Mummy would know she was keeping him waiting. He had put on his priest shirt and collar. He always drives like that so he won't get a ticket if he gets caught speeding.

Monica Faithful Imagine driving away from the house you grew up in, where your parents lived for almost fifty years, for the last time. The last time Eleanor and Jimmy and I would be under that roof together. And just as I really was going out the door, Nora came down the stairs with a box she'd found under a bed on the third floor. It was full of jewelry carved out of lava from Pompeii that somebody bought in Italy a hundred years ago. There were letters too, and photographs bound in a little Victorian album. Whose? Eleanor said she couldn't even look at it. She told Nora to put it in the car and she'd deal with it at home.

We were all out of time. Everything in the house that we were keeping had colored stickers so the movers knew who to ship it all to. Jimmy and his family had already left for the airport; Edie was going to New York with Sylvie. Bobby and Nora were in the den reading old letters while Eleanor tried to make them stop and seal the boxes so she could pack the car.

The piano movers were in the driveway, carrying Papa's Steinway out of the studio to take it to the showroom in New York. Edie said that Charlesie had gotten into Mother's medicine cabinet and started taking the pills. In the end, as I got into the car Norman was talking about how far he wanted to get by nightfall, and I forgot to even look back.

I dream about that house. On my deathbed I'll be able to walk into any room in it and tell you exactly what it looks like; what's on the walls, what's in the drawers.

I hear the family that bought it ripped out the kitchen to make a great room, and put gold-plated faucets in all the bathrooms. They have four children, all girls. They send us Christmas cards.

·II·

ANCIENT AND MODERN HISTORY

How long does it take before you begin to move, leaving behind the world you knew? Three days, just as you thought. But time is rather different here, if we can be said to have it at all, so that answer may not mean what it seems.

So many think that they will slip out of the body and whisk straight away to Heaven or Hell, singing or snarling. But no. There is much to be determined in the spirit world. The spirits of infants and children need time to become themselves. We tend them. Many others arrive with wounds or scars suffered in life in various personal collisions; these are meaningless in celestial terms. Here they are gradually unlearned. And all those bodily aspects that shape the spirit: beauty, ugliness, health or wealth or their lack, all those worldly accidents. What happens when the marks they made are sloughed off? Something slightly different for every soul, and every single variation forms part of the endlessly re-forming universe.

The celestial kaleidoscope. An infinite pattern in which every fleck contains a whole life, and that life is made up of infinite previous lives, a pattern made in dimensions for which there are no words. Eternally absorbing, we understand. In Heaven they watch the celestial kaleidoscope. Here we watch the separate lives.

Lindsay Tautsch Father Faithful rarely sang the mass, which was one of the problems at Good Shepherd. Not the only one or even the most important, but he didn't take it seriously that people minded. They *did* mind in the choir loft, and on the altar guild. The liturgy committee. Another was that Norman chose the hymns. He entertained requests, but he rarely responded to them. He said that if you're six feet five you don't have to.

It's a big rich parish, Good Shepherd Episcopal in Sweetwater, Pennsylvania. For many priests it would be a plum, a career-topper. But for Norman, it was a consolation prize. He'd expected to be a bishop. He has no idea why he isn't. He has a list of published books to his credit. He had his own TV show in Colorado. He's probably the only priest in the communion who contributed a chapter to a textbook on torts.

You can still see the lawyer in him. He loves argument. The clash of battle, the thrill of being cornered, enjoying the mess of fighting his way out of it. He certainly doesn't turn the other cheek to anyone. He did keep a picture of Martin Luther King on the wall in his office, though.

George Kersey When we were in Missouri at the start of our careers, we belonged to a curates' group. We'd meet for supper once a month and tell war stories. I was in a big parish with two curates and a seminarian, but Norman was in a small parish serving a rector who was way past his prime.

A parish can't fire a rector, he has to be removed for cause by his bishop, but the bishop and Norman's rector were old golf buddies, so that wasn't happening. Father Tom was dug in at St. Gregory's with the wagons circled and the loyal church secretary had taken on the role of Rin Tin Tin. Norman and Monica were the Apaches howling outside the stockade with their recruited army of New People while Father Tom huddled in his chair, but Mrs. Snelling could trot in and out among the enemy, swift to sniff out predatory markings and able to carry the bad news back into the fort. When she went home in the evenings she took the print ball from the typewriter with her. Norman still had to type up the order of service and the announcements for the bulletin insert. He had to get his own print ball.

Monica Faithful I loved our parish in Missouri. There was a small college nearby, and Norman started recruiting on campus. There had been no Protestant outreach there at all, though there was a Catholic youth group. Norman would talk to the students about civil rights, he'd tell the stories of Jesus against the Establishment, turning over the tables of the moneylenders in the temple, that kind of thing.

Father Tom was semi-horrified when all these young people started showing up at St. Gregory's on Sunday morning. They'd sit there in their tie-dyed T-shirts expecting Norman to preach. Some of them were black. It was after a couple of boys tried to turn over the army recruiter's table on campus that Mrs. Snelling started taking home the print ball from the Selectric. To try to sideline Norman, Father Tom made him take the children's service, knowing that Norman didn't believe in that, he believed the children should come to worship with everyone else.

Norman Faithful Missouri was fun. My rector hadn't had a new idea in decades and times were a-changing. When Father Tom gave me the children's service, which was nothing short of curate abuse, I started inviting town leaders to come in to talk to the children. One morning the fire chief came, all kitted out in his waterproofs and his red hat, to talk about fire safety. Remember Stop, Drop, and Roll, how they teach you that in grade school? He thought they probably knew that one so he said to the children, "Now what would you do if your clothes were on fire?" And a little girl said indignantly, "Well, I wouldn't put them on!" Word spread that we were having fun, and the grown-ups started coming to the children's service—poor Father Tom.

Monica Faithful Father Tom wasn't very well. He probably wanted to retire, but he was damned if he was going to quit the field once Norman arrived. People began to be afraid he'd die in the pulpit. Luckily, Norman was called to a church of his own, in Oregon. Of our own, I should say. They definitely thought they got me for free when they paid Norman. They were not interested in a rector's wife who had her own life.

Betty Kersey I was sorry when the Faithfuls left—Monica was a lovely person and she'd just started teaching at the elementary school. She'd made friends. Another one of the gals, Selina, her husband had just taken over his first parish, was having a difficult pregnancy. She'd been ordered to bed for two months. That was hard because she should have been out making friends, building her community. Monica used to go over after school and keep her company, or pitch in for her if the altar guild didn't polish the patens right or iron the purificators. People notice every little thing that isn't perfect when you're new, and whatever goes wrong is your fault.

Ted Wineapple A rule of thumb we all learn: in a new parish, beware the people who meet you at the door. They'll be the ones who think they own the place.

Selina Malecki There was something of a war on in our altar guild. On one side was a pair of young moms who'd gone to college back east and didn't wear brassieres. We weren't sure they wore any underwear at all. They insisted their husbands serve on the altar guild. They wanted a woman appointed senior warden, you see, and this was their way of forcing Geoff's hand, even though the older members would hate it if he gave in. Remember *Our Bodies, Ourselves*? That was the bible they worshipped. I'm sure they wouldn't have come to church at all, except they wanted their children in Sunday school.

Well, the men couldn't iron for beans, and the altar guild was all jumpy. Monica came one day, and thank God she stopped in the church before she came over to me. The altar was all decked out with pine boughs and holly and the green burse and chalice veil, and they had set out the green chasuble and stoles—it was Christmas week! She redressed the whole altar for me. Can you imagine?

White is the liturgical color for Christmas. We don't use green until after First Epiphany.

Betty Kersey I remember when Norman was interviewing for that parish in Oregon. The search committee used to call at the strangest hours, just to ask Norm a few more questions—like at eleven o'clock at night. Once Norman and Monica got there, they learned that their last priest had had a problem with the bottle. The vestry wanted to make sure Norman was sober after dinner. People are always guarding against the bad thing that already happened to them, aren't they?

George Kersey I once worked in a school where they'd had a really pugnacious head. He couldn't get along with anyone, although he'd come with great recommendations. Turns out the last school gave him glowing recs because they wanted to get rid of him. He was one of those guys who's great at campaigning for the job, but not so good at doing it.

Anyway, the board fired him. I think it was pretty expensive for them too; he was also good at negotiating his contracts. They hired a guy who seemed perfect, great education, great experience. But he was all soft, he couldn't fire anybody, and that's what you need a new head to do. Move fast to sweep out the deadwood the old head was protecting. This guy knew who needed to go, but he couldn't pull the trigger. All too apt a metaphor. It turned out that the reason he'd left his last school was, he'd fired the art teacher and she came in the next day and shot him.

Kendra Brayton (formerly of Sand Hills, Oregon) Of course I remember the Faithfuls. That was a case of Loved Him, Hated Her. It was a split vote before the congregation called them at all. The other candidate was from California, much more our kind of person, and his wife was cute as a bug. What *were* their names?

Trinny Biggs I was in favor of the guy from Pasa Robles. But Norm preached better, and that carried the day. He was a tall man. When he was all decked out in his robes he looked like God himself.

Right away he started an outreach program to pull in the "unchurched," as he put it. He started lots of new things. That business of hugging and kissing at the Sharing of the Peace? That was new. I was the organist, so no one had to come hug and kiss me, except once in a while someone from the choir got carried away. He started a youth group. He drew the young and then some of their parents started coming, and some others in the village complained that he was poaching Presbyterians. Oh, he preached against war, and he had us all singing Negro spirituals. Not everyone liked it, but there's always going to be some, when you change things.

I thought he was fine. *She* was a cold fish.

Kendra Brayton I was told she was Swedish. Nicky. Maybe that explains it. She didn't take to us, and it was mutual. I remember at the first potluck supper they gave at the rectory, Cassandra Wheat brought her molded salad, and Nicky picked all the little marshmallows out of hers and left them on the side of the plate. Cassandra noticed, believe me. We all did.

Monica Faithful Oregon was not a happy time for me at first. Sand Hills was very pretty; it was apple-growing country, and the church itself was lovely, stone, with a square bell tower like an English country church. But it was in the middle of nowhere and it had been hard, leaving all those friends in Missouri. Not so much for Norman, because he had the new job, and he'd won the competition to get it. I was leaving my friends and I hadn't won anything, and the week we were moving in, I had a miscarriage.

There were these women from the church at the rectory, "helping" me unpack our boxes. They were ripping into things, couldn't wait to see what we had, and they kept putting the china and stuff away wherever they wanted, wherever the last rector's wife would have put it, without letting me stop and think where I wanted things to go. I was having savage cramps and then I went to the bathroom and under my skirt I was all bloody. I sat there weeping while my...it...all went into the toilet. There was *so* much blood. And then there wasn't any toilet paper. I didn't even have a doctor in town yet. For a while I kept bursting into tears, and it was weeks before I could find anything in the kitchen.

Norman Faithful Of course it was a dream come true, to finally have my own parish. The congregation was small and gray when I came, but not for long. I did a youth program at the Y, where the kids played guitars and we sang "Kum ba ya" and all that, and I had myself invited to local schools to meet the kids and preach and pray. I'm told that the minister at the Methodist church went around calling me That Damned Used-Car Salesman. That got a good laugh in the vestry. We were selling the Good News, and people were buying.

Monica Faithful Being the rector's wife is different from being the curate's. The parish feels entitled to you. They'd invite me to ladies' lunches and it was all I could do to sit there. There was a group of widows and never-marrieds who ran a Circle Supper we were supposed to attend. Twice I "forgot" to go. Well, truth: once I really forgot and once I couldn't face it. Norman didn't mind, he does fine with a bevy of hens all clucking over him, but the circle minded, trust me. But I couldn't help it. For them, comfort was an evening of chatter; for me it was a silent house and a Trollope novel I hadn't read before. Then when the circle met at our house I tried to do something fancy out of Julia Child, but I hadn't thawed the chicken enough first, and it was all bloody; no one could eat it.

It didn't help that the previous rector's wife was a saint, a well-known fact. She had twin daughters who'd grown up in the town, both married now with children. One of the daughters came to worship one Sunday unannounced—she and her husband were driving through and made a point to be in Sand Hills for the eleven o'clock. During the Peace, half the congregation left their seats to go hug and kiss pretty little Nettie and her children. After the coffee hour on Sundays, I led a book club with bag lunch; I'd inherited it from Nettie's sainted mother. I'd spent that week reading *Quo Vadis*. Have you read that? It's 561 pages long. I sat there in the parish hall with my big fat book and my list of discussion points and my tuna fish sandwich in a brown bag and not one person came. Not one. They were all down the street at the Coffee Bean having a high old time with Nettie and her family. Even Norman went!

Jeannie Israel I didn't know how depressed Nika was after the miscarriage until she told me on the phone she'd asked her mother to visit her. Sending Sydney to see Monica in a wounded state would have been like asking a tiger to nurse a rabbit with its foot in a trap. Fortunately, Sydney begged off. She must have known she'd be found alone in the house with blood and fur in her whiskers. She did sometimes know her own weaknesses. Not that Monica read it that way.

Monica Faithful Jeannie came out to spend a week with me. God bless her. All you really need is one friend. I told her I hated Sand Hills and it would never come right. We took long hikes, and we laughed, and she helped me see that I'd lost friends and a baby and that was what was wrong, not the fact that Trinny Biggs played by ear instead of reading the music, so if you tried to read the alto line and sing harmony, you couldn't. Actually Trinny wasn't even an organist; it was good of her to fill in. She could play piano, but the only way she could play the organ was if her ex-husband arranged the stops for her.

Kendra Brayton Nicky Faithful went to work in the elementary school in the fall, and I understand she did better there. She was a sub and a tutor and she made great friends with the fourth-grade teacher, Evan Angle, who I always thought was light in his loafers. They were both lonely and they say there's a lid for every pot. You'd see them down at the Coffee Bean laughing away many evenings. You might have thought she'd be home cooking her husband's dinner or starting a family but I suppose she was a women's libber. I wonder what happened to Evan Angle. After the Faithfuls left he moved away too. Went to San Francisco, probably. Isn't that where those people go?

Trinny Biggs Norman was a sweet, sweet man. People went to him for counseling. There was a psychologist in the next town, but people preferred to go to Norman, even some from different churches. He was always willing to get involved. I remember when the Barbers' baby died of crib death. People always blame the parents in those cases. They should have put the baby on her stomach to sleep, or on her back, or let her sleep in the same bed with them, or something. I remember people talked. But Norman got them through it. He just believed in the goodness of the Lord's plan for all of us. "He reminded me that God knows what it is to lose a child," Dodie Barber said to me. I remember that, it gave her such comfort.

Kendra Brayton I was shocked when they left. We wanted a rector who would put down roots here. We'd made that clear. I suppose it was because the wife wanted something grander. Still, it was a rude surprise that all the time we were getting comfortable with them and making them so welcome, they were entertaining better offers. I don't think the fellow from Paso Robles would have done that. I even made some inquiries to see if he was still free, but he was settled somewhere in New England. Off the Faithfuls went to Colorado, with the capital campaign for the new carillon just getting started. Instead of finishing that, we had to start a rector search all over again. We got the carillon finally but it left a taste in the mouth, if you know what I mean.

Trinny Biggs Evan Angle told me that Nicky Faithful's father was a famous pianist at one time. Longhair music. I suppose that explains something.

Kendra Brayton Of course, in Colorado their star started rising. We were just a stepping-stone to them. I remember one Sunday morning my little grandson came into the kitchen and told me, "Mopsy, come quick, God's on television." I went and there was Norman Faithful in full regalia, preaching at the Cathedral of St. John the Divine in New York City. He had written a book, I guess, and had gone to New York to be a celebrity. Booming away in the pulpit about the power of prayer, which was what his book was about, with this huge sea of dressed-up people sitting below him, gazing up.

Monica Faithful When Norman told me he'd been called to Denver, but he wasn't going to uproot me again so soon if I didn't want him to, I didn't even answer. I just went up to the attic and brought down the suitcases. I was pregnant with Edith at the time.

Betty Kersey Denver was a much better place for Norman than Boondocks, Oregon. He's a political animal. He likes the fray. We never did; that's why George left the ministry. George says he's going to write a TV series called *Desperate Rectors*. In Denver Norman became a media darling. He'd get himself on the Sunday morning programs talking about social issues and pretty soon they gave him a show of his own. Every week after church a camera crew would follow him into the rectory and there would be Monica, in her Sunday best, sitting beside him with her ankles crossed, and when she was old enough, Edie too, blinking in the lights. Norman would do this sort of fireside chat about God in the world that week. Once in a while he'd throw a softball question to Monica to answer. He loved the whole thing. There he was, with his perfect little family, leading a perfect Christian Life for all to see.

Bud Shatterman I was on the committee that called Norman to St. John's, and we became great friends. Great friends. He had his strengths, he had his weaknesses, like anybody. But you'll remember, those were the days when people were saying that God was Dead. Young people were falling away from the church, they were going off to India and chanting in Sanskrit. We had a beautiful old sanctuary built for a more prosperous neighborhood than we were any more. It needed a lot of work, and we needed some warm bodies in the pews, we couldn't just expect the old families to pay for it all. Norman understood the problem, and he said he could handle it, and by God he was right. That TV show, that was a hell of a thing. I don't think he prepared for it more than five minutes. He liked the pressure. They just turned the camera on him and he started to talk. It was always a performance. The women were crazy about him.

Clara Thiele I was on the stewardship committee. Normally people hate Stewardship Sunday, but his first year with us, Norman gave a sermon about prosperity consciousness that I still remember. And when we started the campaign to replace the roof, he was an animal. He loved doing the Ask. Bud and I would prepare the soil, and together we'd decide how much to hit each person up for, then we'd send Norman in there and he'd raise the number and close the deal and leave with a check in his hand. And people thanked him for coming!

Sandy Thiele My mom is kind of the pope of the congregation. She loved Mrs. Faithful because she's Danish on her father's side. Thiele's a Danish name. There are a number of Danish families in the congregation who came here after the war, and Mrs. Faithful's aunt was in the Resistance. I used to babysit for Edie, and Mrs. Faithful would tell me about Denmark. I've never been there.

Bud Shatterman Norman hit it off with the bishop too. The bishop wasn't happy about all the ashrams and zendos and whatnot springing up everywhere. His daughter had shaved her head and started calling herself Sachidananda. The bishop made the mistake of preaching against "rotting Eastern religions" one time, and his daughter wrote an angry letter to the *Rocky Mountain News* that they printed. It took a while to calm that down. Norman never had time for meditation or any of that stuff, he was an action guy, an "open your mouth and let God speak through you" guy. Of course sometimes after he'd had a couple of belts he'd open his mouth and say things that were just as silly as the rest of us. But he had such self-confidence, and was always so sure he was forgiven in advance. He charmed you. And all of a sudden, when other churches were floundering, we had a dog in the fight. The Presbyterians and the United Presbys hadn't spoken to each other in decades; they had to combine congregations and sell off one of the sanctuaries. There are expensive condos in it now; I have to shake my head every time I drive by. Meanwhile, we had a thriving church school, and a new roof, and had started raising money to fix the pipe organ.

Ted Wineapple When he'd been in Denver for four or five years, I began to understand how ambitious Norman was. It wasn't just the TV show. He wrote articles for the church papers; he got himself on committees for the national church, he presented at church conferences. I remember a night in Atlanta, after an NNECA convention. He'd gotten a standing ovation. We stayed up into the wee hours with our friend Jack Daniel's. I hadn't known him to drink like that when we were at seminary, but some people respond to applause that way; he was wired. At about two in the morning, he said to me, "Ted, do you think I should go back to New York? That's where the media is. That's where you can really make your mark."

I wondered what kind of mark he meant to make—did he want to be a sportscaster or something? A talk-show host?

Monica Faithful Edith was in third grade, so we'd been in Colorado almost ten years when Norman began to think about New York. The dean at St. John the Divine was a friend, and he told Norman of a church in the Village whose rector was retiring. It wasn't a rich parish but old and fairly famous, and it was very beautiful, the church itself very spare and pure, almost like a Congregational. We flew back there to attend a service incognito before he decided to try for it. Well, as incognito as you can be when you're six five and you never met a camera you didn't like.

The church was fine, except the service was lower than we're used to. Norman must have thought he could change that when he ran the zoo. What I remember was staying with Jeannie, and sitting up half the night talking, manna from heaven. The idea of living close to her again! And of being only a day's drive from Dundee, and being able to visit my parents or my sister without putting the dog in the kennel and flying for a whole day . . .

Norman Faithful The thing that drove that decision was Edie and Nicky. Edie was having trouble at her school in Colorado. There was some sort of click she'd been left out of, one of those things girls go through, but it wasn't good for her. The New York church had a school attached, a sweet little place, where Edie could go for half tuition. Plus, I was worried about Sam and Sylvie. We'd had them in the summers, but I couldn't get east for more than two weeks, and they were beginning to feel like strangers to me. So I put my hat in the ring, and went to New York and preached my heart out. It was no cakewalk. New York doesn't usually take to Westerners. I did have something of a national presence and a strong track record at raising money, which they badly needed. They flew the whole family in *twice* to look us over.

In the end, they not only hired me, they hired Nicky to teach second grade. So Edie got to go to the school for free. The rectory was a tiny little shambles of a house but it was delightful. We missed the big backyard and having a separate study for Nicky. But I was ready for a new challenge and I rolled up my sleeves and waded in.

Sylvia Faithful It's *clique,* not *click.* I tried to tell him that once, but he just looked at me, and then went on talking as if I hadn't said anything.

Ted Wineapple I was pleased to have my old friend in the East again. I was in Richmond at the time. And I was very happy for Monica. She was so grateful to be back where she knew the names of the trees and the birds.

Monica Faithful In the West it takes you a long time to realize that it's not only that you're new in town ... you will *never* be walking down the street and run into someone you grew up with or knew from school. You will always feel as if you're on a tightrope without a net. You'll make new friends, but you'll never be as important to them as they are to you. And you'll never speak that shorthand together that comes from sharing common points of biography.

Ted Wineapple It was a lesser parish, with many more problems than the one he was leaving. A church with a school attached? You have no idea. Especially a church that's failing while the school succeeds.

It was better for Monica. She looked happier than she had in years, still fairly slim, with some gray in her hair, but something lighter and clearer in her eyes. It was better for Edith, much better for Sam and Sylvie. Worse for Bridey, who'd had a big backyard in Colorado, but that wouldn't have weighed with Norman. I think they still had Bridey then, the border terrier. (The only time I ever personally saw Monica push back against Norman in public was right after Bridey's mother was hit by a car and killed, and Norman declared that dogs don't have souls.)

Anyway, there's no doubt in my mind that the reason Norman took Holy Innocents was, he thought if he could pull off another coup like his Denver miracle, and in the Big Apple, the next step was the cathedral chair.

Monica Faithful The rectory was this small little nineteenth-century row house behind the church. Probably worth a fortune now but New York City was pretty rough in those years. Graffiti was everywhere. Our front door got bombed so many times we gave up repainting it. Bombing is what the graffiti kids called it. Bombing. Tagging. And the house was drafty and all out of plumb. If you put a marble down on the parlor floor, it rolled to the other side of the room.

And, there were mice. It had wide-plank old pine floors with great gaps between them, all full of mouse dirt. We couldn't have a cat because Norman's allergic. We couldn't put down poison for fear Bridey would eat it. We had to trap them. For all that happened to us while we were at Holy Innocents, my clearest association is walking into that cold kitchen in my bathrobe in the mornings, with the wind shaking the windowpanes, listening for the scrabbling sound behind the refrigerator that meant a mouse was in the trap and it wasn't dead. If you think Norman was going to deal with that sort of thing, good luck to you.

Edith Faithful I liked Holy Innocents School pretty much. We had smaller classes. There was good art. All the other kids had known each other since they were three, so that was hard for me, and our play yards were tiny and I liked sports. One was a fenced-in lot beside the school and the other was up on the roof. That was for the little kids. It was a kindergarten-through-sixth-grade school. After sixth, you went to public middle school, or changed to one of the private schools that went through twelfth. The gym wasn't very big and it was also used for plays and assembly. I loved being able to go home for lunch. Dad would make me soup and Triscuits, or tomato sandwiches, and we both read at the table while we ate. We weren't allowed to do that when Mom was there.

Ted Wineapple Norman hadn't had a failure since he was five, that I could tell. Oh yes. I guess you could say his marriage to Rachel had failed. Though I'm not sure he saw it that way. When he got to New York, it happened that the senior warden, who'd been there forever, was recovering from surgery. He asked Norman to have the vestry meet at his apartment, instead of in the parish hall, and Norman said, "Of course." Big mistake.

Monica Faithful Being in the faculty room, in on the gossip, I understood the parish better than I would have otherwise, and maybe better than Norman did. The parish and the school were at war with each other. Absolute war. The school was coining money. Downtown New York was changing, there were people living in places like SoHo that had never been residential before and there suddenly weren't enough schools for the downtown kids.

Holy Innocents School could have been twice as big as it was, but it was bonsaied by the church. Some of the class-rooms were actually in the church undercroft and the base-ment of the parish hall. They had to be completely cleaned up, all the displays and maps and so forth put away every Friday, so the rooms could be used for Sunday school over the weekend. Even when no one came to Sunday school, the vestry made us do that. The rest of the school buildings were this little jumble on church land that had grown up higgledy-piggledy. The school wanted to tear them down and build a suitable building, and take the meditation gar-den, which nobody used, for more play yards. The vestry was dead set against it.

The vestry looked at the school as a cash cow, period. If there was a budget shortfall at the church, and there always was, they made the school cover it. It caused havoc with the school budget. And school fund-raising. People didn't want to give toward a new theater curtain or piano for the music room if the church was just going to come and take the money.

Norman Faithful I was writing a book about the urban church. I joined a group of prominent clergy marching to protest the blight in the South Bronx. The dean of the ca-thedral allowed me to preach up there now and then, and I got several op-ed pieces published in the *Times*. You'd have thought all of that would draw parishioners to Holy Inno-cents, but it didn't.

Location was a problem. The unchurched in the neighborhood were old lefties with no interest in established religions, and the young families either weren't interested in Christianity or weren't interested in joining a church with the kind of financial problems Holy Innocents had. I thought it would be easy to draw families who had children in our school, but that too was not meant to be. I spent a lot of time on my knees that first year or two.

Monica Faithful Norman tried to start a youth group, which had always been one of his strong suits, but at Holy Innocents, he couldn't get it off the ground. He was older and didn't look hip or cool as he had in Oregon or when we first got to Colorado. And New York teenagers are not like kids in other places. They have subways, they can move around the city without having to drive so they're not stuck at home or prowling the mall bored out of their squashes. Sitting in a parish hall or the rector's study with someone who reminded them of their parents didn't strike them as an entrancing way to spend an evening. Why should it, when they could as soon be out on the street with cans of spray paint, writing their tags on people's front doors? "Kum ba ya" was definitely over.

Meanwhile, the vestry was wilding.

Norman Faithful Hi Thomas was the senior warden. He'd been ill, and he asked me to bring the vestry to him for my first meeting. Seemed like a sensible request. But the anti-Thomas faction, and there was bound to be one, I realized too late, decided that meant I was Hi's creature.

The church was hemorrhaging money when I got there.

Hi didn't see it as a problem. The school makes plenty of money. The anti-Thomas faction wanted to rent the sanctuary to a church called St. Jude's that had no home of its own for a nine o'clock service. Only about six people come regularly to ours. But of course, those six were addicted to their little service and their little time slot, and one of them was Hi Thomas's wife. St. Jude's saw themselves as the early Christians, pure and persecuted. They were Anglo-Catholics, mostly confirmed bachelors, and they used the 1928 prayer book. The Episcopal church is a big tent, but not big enough for St. Jude's under our roof, according to Hi Thomas. They'd fill the place with smells and bells, they'd bow at the Incarnatus, and other abominations.

In the middle of all this, I had to tell the vestry we didn't want to live in the rectory.

Monica Faithful There was one night when Edith literally gasped for breath; she couldn't even get enough to call to me, but she woke me anyway, it was so loud and desperate. I called 911. We spent six hours in the ER, frightened out of our wits. Did you know asthma could come on so suddenly? Well, the upshot was that it was the mouse dirt in the house that was making her sick. One hundred fifty years of it. Mice were in the walls and under the floors. The docs said she could live in a sterile tent in her room, or we could move.

Bella McChesney I never thought Norman Faithful was committed to us. From the first he was like one of those people at a cocktail party who is looking over your shoulder to see if someone more important has come in.

Paul McChesney When they first arrived, we had them to dinner. I wanted to give him some advice, you know. Give him the lay of the land, tell him what he might want to watch out for. He wasn't listening. He was very entertaining, I give him that. He told some wild story about a colleague whose church was haunted by the former rector. If you went into the nave at midnight there were noises and blasts of cold air. Lights that had been out were found burning in the morning. He and his friend went in there together and performed some kind of exorcism.

After they left, Bella said that Norman had drunk over half a bottle of very expensive Scotch. I should have known he was already in bed with Hi Thomas.

Ted Wineapple I never thought Norman should be a bishop. He was too much of a lone wolf. And I thought the royal trappings would be spiritually dangerous for him. The first step toward becoming a bishop should be a great deal of very humble prayer, a great deal of "Thy will, Lord, not mine." To be sure that it is God calling you to the bishopric, and not your own ego. The higher you go in the church, the harder it is to tell which line your calls are coming in on.

But something in the heart of man loves a hierarchy. A pyramid, having it there, and climbing it. This is a church we've built in the name of one who said, "When two or three are gathered in my name . . ." Two or three. In private, with no display and no audience, just two or three, in faith. This is a church of very poor listeners.

Monica Faithful There was a time when I knew Jesus as a person, a man like my father or my brother, who had me by the hand—who knew and cared about me as a person, who listened for my voice in the night and found ways to answer me, showed me his love in the eyes of a friend, spoke to me, from pulpits, from books, from the mouths of children. He was alive and He was with me. To have had that and lost it is . . . I can't finish this sentence.

Ted Wineapple Norman told me once about the moment he decided to be a priest. He and Monica were on some island in Maine, poking around an old settlement that had vanished, when he heard somebody weeping. No one was there. He said it was a woman. He said it seemed to be pleading with him for something, comfort, attention, something. And he knew in that instant that he could help, that God wanted him to help.

Have you made any sort of study of ghost stories? I have. Not *The Turn of the Screw*, not the kind made up by authors. I mean the kinds of contacts that happen to real people. I do happen to believe the spirit world is thick around us. How could I not? But I'll tell you something about those stories. For one thing, there are more of them in places close to water. Islands. I have no idea why, I'm just observing. For another, by far the most common are of furious servants or slaves or victims. People who could not express their rage in life at what life had given to others but not to them. Would you seek such souls if they had bodies?

I asked Norman that, and in about ten seconds flat he was off on a tear about starting a writing program for angry people in prisons. I mean—he wasn't *wrong*, but that wasn't the point.

❦

Islands. Interesting.

Of course we are involved with those in the body. The air around you is crowded with us.

How we concern ourselves with you is stage eight or nine at least. There have been those in the body who have grasped it, but usually even here it takes individual tutorial. One can't even ensnare it in body language without using a body word like that "individual." Since that particular personal individual thing one spends so much time protecting becomes useless here as the egg shell to the hatchling. The great relief, the great good thing about here, is that you don't have to now protect and honor both at once, the shell and the spirit maturing inside. All those uncomfortable dualities. Art versus science. Mind versus body. Good versus evil. Becoming versus being. One yearned for the simplicity of being all one thing. Here it is.

❦

Norman Faithful The diocese of Hawaii was seeking a bishop coadjutor. It was perfect. It was as if the Lord said to me, through my child's desperate struggle for breath, Take your family to a new place, where it's pure and warm and you can all heal. There you will find a mentor to help you grow into the miter and the crozier. This is what I have trained you for. Here you will be my good shepherd, and use your highest gifts.

Bella McChesney I made an appointment with Norman. I told Paul I was going to do it. I thought it might help him to hear what people were saying if it came from a woman, since he seemed to get along with them so well. He chose the time, and I met him in his office in the parish hall.

I'd arrived a little early and put my head in at the sacristy, since it was open, just to be sure all was well in that department. Things have not always been perfect in appearance since Father Faithful came. There was a stain on his alb you could see from the fifth row one week, and sometimes the ushers failed to straighten up the pews after services, and I had to go through them gathering bulletins and putting the hymnals back in the racks. Which I'm happy to do, of course. But Norman came to the door of the sacristy and stood looking at me as if it wasn't my business to be in there, which I didn't like.

I'd brought him a stole I'd been working for some time, with Greek crosses in gold thread. Actually I started it for Father Andrew and then left off when he was so rigid about the Women's Committee. When I knew he was leaving, I got it out and finished it for the new rector. I'm a past president of our chapter of the Embroiderers' Guild of America, so you may take it my work is excellent.

Father Norman unwrapped the package and I could see he was very touched. He thanked me; then he asked me to pray with him that he would wear my gift in humility and gratitude, for God's love and for the chance to serve in our parish, amen. It was slickly done. I told him how much we were enjoying his beautiful preaching, and how much we hoped that our work together would be long and fruitful, as we were so lucky that he had answered our call. He seemed pleased. Then I told him what he needed to hear.

I said, "Father Norm, there's something I feel I should share with you as I know there are quite a few in the congregation who have this concern. Have expressed distress and dismay, in fact."

"About what?" he said.

I said, "We're an old parish, as you know. Some of our families have worshipped here for many generations, and we may be a little set in our ways. But that's not always a bad thing."

"Bella," he said, "is this about the rectory?"

He looked as if he thought it was funny. He interrupted me and thought it was funny.

I was very smooth. I don't think he had the least idea that he'd made me angry. But really, where were *his* people four generations ago?

I said, "The rectory has served six leaders of this parish, and their families, for over one hundred and twenty years. We believe that it's one of the treasures of Holy Innocents."

"So do I," said Norm. "I thank God you have been such wise stewards as to possess a piece of real estate that makes it possible for a priest to live in your parish without robbing a bank."

I waited, since obviously there was a But coming.

"But my daughter has had an asthma attack that nearly killed her. We were advised by her doctors to move her and, as she's only ten, she really cannot live alone."

He thought he was being amusing. I said, "I've heard your reasons; you forget my husband sits on the vestry."

"I never ever forget that," he said.

I said a really thorough professional cleaning would take care of the problem. He said he thought so too. With a thorough cleaning the rectory could be rented for enough money to cover the Faithfuls' rent in a clean new building, and probably leave some over for the general fund.

I said the parish would be deeply distressed to have the rector living far from the church, where they don't know where to find him. "You forget," I said, "this church once burned to the ground and was rebuilt by the vast generosity of a few loyal members." Including my husband's grandfather, I did not say. But I did say, "That fire would not have gone undetected had the rector been in residence at the rectory instead of in France on holiday."

He pointed out that the same thing could happen if he lived in the rectory; a fire could break out and he wouldn't notice as he'd be in the hospital nursing his daughter.

I won't go on. It was outrageous, really. I was trying to help him. I was trying to tell him what people were saying. It was not the kind of reception I expected. I honestly think some people go into the priesthood because they are little tinhorn dictators. They love the thrill of standing in the pulpit decked out like saints, while people gaze adoringly and hand over power to them that belongs, by rights, to God. I went home and said to Paul, this is it. I mean it. I'm going to transfer back to Grace Church or try St. Luke's.

Monica Faithful After we moved back to the East Coast I saw my parents fairly often. Papa had kept his pied-à-terre in New York. He wasn't performing as much as when he was younger, but he loved playing chamber music with old friends and he loved teaching at Mannes. Mother belonged to the Cosmopolitan Club. When she came into town by herself she stayed there. That's interesting, isn't it? She didn't stay at Papa's apartment. Maybe they both needed their retreats from each other. Maybe all marriages do.

Norman Faithful You ask the search committee for their package, the profile of the diocese, job description, and application. You fill that out and write a heartfelt letter explaining why you would make a splendid bishop, and you get your letters of recommendation. Then you wait to see if you'll make the final cut. Four of us made it; I was called to Honolulu for the "walkabout" in April.

Honolulu! The air was so soft, the birds and flowers were like jewels. I'd had a ticket for the back of the bus, which was going to be quite a spiritual test, since it's more than ten hours in the air, altogether. But I wore my black shirt and round collar, and at the last minute the girl at the gate upgraded me. I blessed her. I have a suspicion she thought I was Catholic, but no harm done. And Honolulu—that was love at first sight. You're shown around the diocese, you meet with various groups, ordained and lay, from the different parishes, and chat and answer questions. In the end they gave us all the same topic and we preached on it.

❧

Monica Faithful I was meeting Mother at the Cos Club for lunch. Mother was all in a fuss and flurry over Norman becoming a bishop. She seemed to think I'd finally done something right. She wanted to know all about the duties, and what kind of mansion a bishop gets, and what's the tall hat called. She liked pomp. Well, it *was* exciting. I was telling about the investiture, how the new bishop comes to the closed doors of the cathedral and knocks three times, and waits for them to be opened to him. Inside, his new constituents are all waiting in their pews, craning their necks. It's *so* theatrical, which of course would appeal to her.

That's where I was in the story, at the knocking at the doors. In her mind I knew Mother was inside, in the front row with the children and me, waiting to see the sudden sunlight as the doors opened, with Norman's dark figure silhouetted in the middle, then Norman sweeping up the aisle looking eight feet tall in his cope and miter. When I suddenly felt that appalling gush that every woman learns to dread, especially when it's not due. In mid-sentence, I said, "Excuse me, Mother, I'll be right back," and got out of the room as quickly as I could. She was staring, with her fork halfway to her mouth. I couldn't back out of the room, but I wanted to.

I got to the powder room praying that nothing had soaked through yet. In vain. The skirt was stained so badly I knew perfectly well I must have ruined the banquette. I began to cry while I tried to clean the blood off my legs with bathroom tissue, but the stall looked like an abattoir. Then I heard Mother talking to the attendant. The attendant tapped at my door to ask if I needed help. Of course I did, desperately, but what kind? A bath and a change of clothes? A diaper? What the hell was I going to do? Then my mother bugled, "Monica—do you need a doctor?" I said I thought I probably did. She said she'd call mine, what was his name. And of course I couldn't remember. I'd seen him only once. She said, "Oh, for heaven's sake!"

It was horrible. The club sorted it out, found an ob-gyn who would see me immediately. I think one of the ladies in the dining room was a doctor and arranged it. By the time Norman had finished his chats and his speech in Hawaii, I was being scheduled for a hysterectomy. I guess more than one thing had gone wrong that day, though we never understood what. Well, the fibroids we understood. Which is worse, I wonder, for a woman to lose the organ that makes her a woman and a mother? Or a man whose lifework is made of his trust that he knows what he knows, to find out he doesn't?

Norman Faithful How the hell do you grow a thing the size of a cantaloupe in your stomach and not notice it? That's what I want to know.

Jeannie Israel Norman sets off on some grand folly of his own that he's forgotten to thoroughly sort out with his wife, and Nika bleeds into her shoes. A pattern emerges. You'd think her God could work out some other way of getting her attention.

Eleanor Applegate Mother called me. The way she described how embarrassed she was, you'd have thought Monica had deliberately gored her own ox in the middle of the dining room. I went down to stay with Nika until Storming Normal could get back from Hawaii. In any event, I stayed a day or two longer to be with Edie until Nika was home from the hospital and on her feet. She'd been through a lot and was pretty much a wreck at first.

The night Norman got home, he was on West Coast time

and he was very wound up about how things had gone in Hawaii. I think he knew he hadn't nailed it. We stayed up half the night talking. I'd never spent time like that with him, just the two of us, plus there are some people who are nicest after they've been kicked down the stairs. He was very unguarded and human. I quite got the point of him that night.

However, while I was there, I also took a couple of phone calls from no one. You know, if a woman's voice answers, hang up? I don't know that's what they were. They could well have been wrong numbers. But they happened.

Monica Faithful I cried a lot. It took me by surprise, how sad I was, and I never could tell exactly why. Knowing there would really be no more children? It hadn't seemed like it was going to happen, and I don't know how we'd have afforded it if it had, but still. Really understanding I was going to get old and fail and die? And the surgery itself was surprisingly awful. They cut through your abdominal muscles and leave a big scar, and you can't hold your stomach in and it takes forever to get your energy back. I guess there were also hormone things . . . anyway I went to Dundee early that summer, as soon as Edie was out of school. Not fun for her. Someone at school made a joke about her parents, Mr. and Mr. Faithful, and she had to pretend it was funny.

Eleanor Applegate Nika was in rough shape. Depressed. I didn't like the way she sounded on the phone, and Jeannie said she didn't either. It's surprising how an organ you've never seen in your life could mean so much. She wanted to get out of New York, go to Dundee and sit in the sun on the bathing beach with a book, and only talk to people who loved her. She asked Mother if she could stay at Leeway, and Big Syd said no. Can you believe that? The cottage wasn't opened yet and she couldn't put Shirley to the trouble of changing the schedule. (And why, hello, would the housekeeper's convenience be so much more important to her than Nika's?)

I called Shirley and asked her to open *our* house early and of course she was delighted to do it. Everything was ready for Nika two days later. She packed the car and took Edie and the dog and went north.

Monica Faithful That was how I happened not to be in town when the news came from Hawaii. After the finalists preach, there's a diocesan convention with two groups of delegates voting, ordained and lay. They keep it up until one candidate has a majority in both groups. It only took four ballots, and Norman came in third.

Norman Faithful It was all political. I was on the phone with a couple of my supporters, and they went through it vote by vote. Bishop Simmons, who made my nominating speech, had his enemies among the conservatives, and it was felt by some that he'd been so warm in supporting me, I must have promised to make him dean of the cathedral.

Also, I guess, there had been grumbling about my referring to notes during my sermon. I usually don't prepare like that. I usually just pray on my topic for a while beforehand and then get up on my hind legs and see what happens. But I thought it was important to show them I don't always go around doing things by the seat of my pants, since Simmons told me it was a concern he'd heard. I'd prepared that speech like a lawyer. Maybe I wasn't at my best, I don't know. I think it's all politics. The guy they hired came from Iowa but he had worked in the diocese and had friends there.

Monica Faithful It was like running away from home. Bobby and Eleanor's house has no heat except fireplaces, so it was bloody cold at night still. There were blackflies, which I'd heard about but never seen. They get in your eyes and up your nose. I spent a lot of time walking by myself and, I suppose, crying. Edith was adorable but children shouldn't be made to feel responsible for their parents.

Sylvia Faithful I was in New York that year, working and taking classes at the New School. I was waiting on tables at a tiny restaurant in SoHo that was just getting hot. I worked weekend evenings, the best time because it's busiest. But it meant I was up to like four A.M. every Friday and Saturday night, and had no social life of my own at all. Out of the blue, Dad called me and said he was batching it and offered to take me to dinner. I said I'd go if he promised not to show up in his dog collar. I was pleased, actually. I thought maybe this would be a time when we could reconnect.

We went to the NoHo Star, which was kind of my local for after school or after work. My choice. Once we were there I realized it was going to be too loud for Dad. He was beginning to lose his hearing and didn't want to admit it. *Tant pis.*

I didn't really mean to, but I started talking about Mom,

not that he'd asked. Mom has always been kind of high-strung, but lately everything was exaggerated. She was alone too much, she believed things that weren't true. If I called her all the time or went to see her, she came to expect it and lit into me if I missed a day. If I told her I couldn't deal and stayed away, she'd call me up and cry, and tell me she'd been so good, not calling me for six days, that she thought I'd reward her by calling her on the seventh. She thought I knew that was going on in her mind. When she cried it broke my heart and when she attacked me I wanted to hang up on her. Why was her unhappy life *my* problem? Where was everybody else? Where were her sisters, where was Sam? Did she do these things to him? (Answer: no. Sam is a guy. Guys don't like it when women cry, so for him she turns on the charm.) I had just turned twenty-one and no one in my family even noticed.

You want to know something amazing? The only person in my whole family—families—who called me on my birthday was Uncle Jimmy. He called me from California and asked me what I was doing to celebrate. When I told him nothing, he said to get a friend and go to Raoul's on Prince Street. When we got there, he'd called ahead and bought us a bottle of Veuve Clicquot and left us an open tab so we could have dinner and everything. And he'd told them to card me, so soon everyone in the place knew it was my birthday and people kept sending us drinks and we stayed all night. Actually, a great birthday. Go figure.

The more I talked about Mom, the edgier Dad got. He said, "Your mother was always an unhappy woman. I tried to fix it and I couldn't. People choose their paths and if they don't like where it takes them, they have to figure it out." I said, "She didn't choose her path. You chose it for her." He said, "Things happen. If she hadn't been so angry and sad, we might still be together." I said, "If you hadn't slept with someone younger and fancier you might still be together," and he snapped back, "Watch your mouth, Rachel."

Then we stared at each other, hearing what he'd just said. Finally he said, "Sorry, Sylvie. I know you and your mother are very different people."

But does he?

Norman Faithful The day I got the call from Honolulu, I was stunned, frankly. I didn't want to be alone. Nicky had taken Edith and gone to Maine. I thought of Sylvia. I hadn't seen nearly enough of her since we'd been back. She was working hard, and seemed to have a lot of friends and a full life, and of course, we'd had a lot of settling in to do, not to mention Lady McChesney and her little power trip, and then there was Edie wheezing away at night. But I thought of all those times when maybe Sylvie had cried in the night and wanted her daddy and I wasn't there. I'd hoped this might be a time to pick up where we left off. But too much had happened to her while I was gone. I liked to think of her as my pink and cream little girl, with her braids and her little beads strung onto her shoelaces, wanting me to read her a story before she could go to sleep.

Sylvia Faithful Every time Dad sees that I'm an adult, an adult who sees through him, he gets this sentimental ex-pression, and I know he's going to start in on some sneakers I had when I was five. I don't even remember the damn things. I'm not really sure they were my sneakers; maybe they were Edie's.

Norman Faithful I reached my hand across the table to hers, and said, "Sylvie. Remember when you were a little girl in pigtails, and—"

Sylvia Faithful I said, "Norman, stop it. I'm a twenty-one-year-old woman. I support myself, I'm getting As in college, you have no idea who I am! You think our whole relationship is me sitting on your lap while you read *Uncle Wiggly*! Get over it! Our whole relationship is me standing around at the coffee hour after church, wanting to blow my brains out, I'm so bored, while you receive your adoring subjects. I'm the one you don't have a single picture of in your living room. You even have pictures of the dog in your living room!"

He looked stunned. He said, "I'm sure that's not true," and I said, "Fine. Bet." I took out five twenties and put them on the table, and the question wasn't worth that much to him, he didn't want to lose a hundred dollars. So he said, "Where did you get so much money?" And I said, "I *earned* it, Dad." And then I couldn't sit still any more. I was afraid I'd start crying or screaming at him, so I left. And I left the money on the table. I could see him through the window as I walked down Lafayette Street toward SoHo. He was still sitting there, staring down at the table as if he didn't know what had just happened to him.

I almost went back in, because he looked confused and sad. But I didn't. I thought, Let him figure it out.

Norman Faithful She never even asked me about Hawaii.

Monica Faithful I stayed in Dundee all that summer. It was the first time since I was little that I'd been there from June to September. It was bliss. I know now that it was a mistake, but I'm still not sure I would go back and change it if I could.

Papa was so glad to have me there. Mother was beginning to repeat herself and be confused. Shirley Eaton had taken over from Ellen Gott, who had retired, and she wasn't used to Mother. I talked her out of quitting two or three times, and by the end of the summer she was so fond of Papa that I knew it would be all right.

I stayed with Eleanor for a couple of days when she came up with Charlesie and Nora over the Fourth. Nora and Edie are almost exactly the same age and they really found each other that summer. When Eleanor's houseguests started arriving, Edie and I moved over to Leeway Cottage. I spent a lot of time in the garden with Mother, and we went sailing with Papa most fine days.

Amelia came up to visit her parents; we had a week together. I read for hours on the porch at Leeway. In August Jeannie came, and all the young began to arrive, Adam and Annie Applegate and Amelia's daughter Barbara. Toby Crane showed up; I hadn't seen him in years. He told me he'd been in love with me when I was fifteen. Unlikely to be true, but sweet of him to say. He and Papa and I cruised down to Camden overnight. Long lazy days and crisp smoky nights. It was just what the doctor ordered.

Norman Faithful All through July, Bella McChesney could be found huddled in groups that would break apart from one another when I approached. Then she began taking notes whenever we spoke. I mean, at the coffee hour! I asked her to come in to talk about her concerns, and when she arrived, she asked if she could tape the conversation. I said I didn't care to talk to an unseen audience, that this was a private meeting for the benefit of two people only. She got up and left.

Monica Faithful Norman was supposed to come up for two weeks in August, but he kept moving the dates and in the end he didn't come at all. I missed him, but not as much as I would have if I'd been anywhere but Dundee. If he holds that against me, I guess he's entitled.

Anyway, I didn't press him. I thought at the time with the McChesney insurrection heating up that he was wise to stay. He found a perfect apartment for us, and I flew down one weekend to see it before he signed the lease. He seemed awfully distracted. But I didn't like leaving Edie alone with Mother, so I didn't stay to sort it out. He had our furniture all moved into the new apartment by the time we got home. Edie never had to spend another night in the mouse house.

The first Sunday we were back in New York, Bella McChesney came up to me at the coffee hour and said, "Your husband's been a busy boy." I said, "Yes, and I'm so grateful to him." She stood looking at me as if deciding whether to answer. I held my ground, even though it was clear she was dying to say more, and finally she walked away. Norman came over and put his arm around me. He said, "I'm glad you're back." I could see why. At least I thought I could.

Sylvia Faithful Monica invited me to dinner the first week
they were back. I could tell Dad hadn't told her about our
little contretemps. I brought a loaf of bread and a box of salt
as a housewarming present. Monica looked puzzled. It's a
Jewish custom; Mom taught it to me, which I told Monica
and she was pleased. I'd also brought a really good bottle of
wine, from the restaurant. It was a hot night, and they had
the windows open so we'd get the evening breeze. The
apartment was on a high floor but you could hear the street
noise, which I liked.

While Monica and Edie were in the little kitchen, getting ready to serve the supper, Dad came over to me and
put an arm around me, and at the same time, slipped something into my jacket pocket. I took it out and looked: my
hundred dollars. He said, "Please take it." Then he looked
over at the bookshelf and I saw there was a picture of me
from my high school graduation in a silver frame. Wearing
my gown and that dorky hat with the tassel. I put the
money into my pocket.

At dinner, Edie and I got into a tickling game. I'd wait
for her to be distracted, then I'd sneak in a tweak in the
ribs. She'd wait for me to be eating and then get me in the
armpit, or try to. We got to giggling and Dad had to say,
"Now, girls!" but he didn't really seem to mind. Edie kept
sneaking looks to see if she could get me again. Then she
said, "What's around your neck, Sylvie?" I took it out and
showed her.

She said it was pretty, and I told her it was jade, and
Monica said, "That looks like a Buddha." I said that it was
one, and Dad put down his fork. He said, "And does it have

special meaning for you, or . . ." I said, "Or is it just jewelry? It has special meaning for me, Dad." He gave me this really long look, and then went back to his dinner.

I said, "You know what, Daddy? Not everything I do is about you." He raised one hand, as if to wave me away, and went on eating.

·III·
NORA'S PHOTO ARCHIVE
(SO FAR . . .)

The Elms. Date?

James Brant.

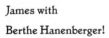

James with
Berthe Hanenberger!

'from where we tee "off" every day.
G.S.B.
J.H.B.

Dundee Golf Association Clubhouse; c. 1912.

Back says: "Sunporch, 1916." I know it's The Elms, but who are these people?
Great-great-grandmother Annabelle in wheelchair,
and we think the very pretty lady is Mrs. Maitland.

Candace Lee (left) with her sister Charlotte. Knoxville.

Candace Lee Brant—engagement picture?

Laurus Moss, 1918 (?)

Annabelle Sydney Brant. On the back in Candace's writing: "ASB, 1919.

Last time she looked anything like a Lee."

Sydney. On back, Candace's writing: "ASB on left. What is she wearing? With Tiny Charlotte. Knoxville, 1926."

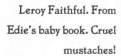

Leroy Faithful. From Edie's baby book. Cruel mustaches!

Henrik and Ditte Moss. Nyborg, Denmark, 1938.

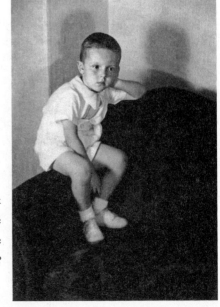

Jimmy Moss. Back
says, "1950." Can we
Photoshop those
shadows?

Eleanor Moss, senior year.

Bobby Applegate. Back says, "Dundee, 1963."

Monica Moss with Annie Applegate.
Thanksgiving in Connecticut, 1968.

Norman Faithful.
Cambridge,
Massachusetts, 1969?

Edith Faithful, left,
in Colorado with her
friend Shannon and the
headmaster's dog.

Sam and Sylvia Faithful. Massachusetts, 1991.

Uncle Jimmy. From silver frame on Sydney's bureau. What year? And what boat is that?

Mom and Dad. (Great picture...)

·IV·
THE SUMMER OF SHARING

There is a cloud of unknowing about Heaven and Hell, apparently. Those forever places, after the spirit work is done. You understand what some of us call karma? The gyre, on which you come around again and again to the same psychic knots or dilemmas you faced before, but always on a different level? So they are the same but changed? Until you learn how to pass through them unscathed?

No?

All right, then. A simpler way of saying it.

No one is "sent" anywhere. You choose. Or find that you have chosen.

There are plenty in Hell, for want of a better word, but they don't know it's Hell. To them, it's just more of what they always chose to believe about how the world works.

Josslyn Moss I know they think I'm a Valley Girl moron. The summer after Jimmy and I were married, I sat through a family dinner where Bobby Assholegate took a quarter out of his pocket, and every time I used the word *like*, he tapped it on the table. What did he think, I didn't notice? He'd be like turned away from me, talking to Monica, and

I'd answer a question and down the table I'd hear that coin click on the table. See? Just telling you that made me say it. Asshole.

The Leeway Cottage Guestbook, August 19, 1988 (Laurus's hand) *We're back from Santa Barbara, where Jimmy and his girl were married on the beach at sunset. Jimmy slew the fatted calf for us. Long layover in Chicago on way home, otherwise, everything perfect.*

Eleanor Applegate Mother was slipping faster by 1988. I don't know if that was the reason, he was trying to spare her having to organize things, or maybe protecting Josslyn, but Jimmy insisted on giving his whole wedding himself. It was just our family and Josslyn's, but we all stayed at the Santa Barbara Biltmore. It has beautiful flowers and palm trees, and the most heavenly view of the Pacific. The kids adored it.

Mother had bought a new dress for the wedding and a big matching hat, and she looked so pretty. We all had to take our shoes off on the beach and walk on the sand in our stockings to where the chairs were set up. Mother was quite girlish and sweet about it. I was just glad I'd had a pedicure. The service was performed by a friend of Jimmy's who was a Universal Life Church minister. You know, a divinity degree you can buy in the mail.

Josslyn Moss We had it timed perfectly, so that the sun went below the horizon just as we said our vows. Then we all walked back to the hotel by the light of torches and had dinner. We didn't have any attendants because my sister

Melaynie is pretty heavyset, and self-conscious about it; it would have been hard to find matching dresses for her and anybody else. We asked Norman to bless our rings, since we weren't going to have him do the service, since we aren't Christians. But he said he doesn't do cameos. I was afraid he was going to be a prick about it, but he was fine. He didn't wear his collar or anything and he said he liked being able to sit with his wife at a wedding for once. They held hands the whole time.

Eleanor Applegate Josslyn's mother was a hoot. Salt of the earth. She'd been married four times and counting and two of her husbands came to the wedding, Josslyn's father and another one, and it was not the one she was married to at the time! You never knew what was going to come out of her mouth. We sat with her at the dinner and she suddenly said to me, "You know, I was seventeen the first time I got married and when the pastor asked me, 'Do you take this man,' I fainted!" Then she roared with laughter. She told me she'd made her own wedding dress out of a tablecloth.

She's spent a lot of time in Reno, getting divorces, and over the years worked out a system for playing blackjack. She plays in the middle of the night, when they're training new dealers. "I win a bundle, honey," she kept saying and then she'd laugh. She was a riot.

Josslyn Moss Every time Mama came back to the table from having a smoke, Mr. Moss would stand up for her. She'd say, "Oh Lars, you don't have to do that." But he did it anyway. After a while my dad started doing it too. So then Mama would say, "You make me feel like a queen!"

Afterward she said that Laurus was a real gent, real old-school, and that we wouldn't see any more like him. He made her feel honored. I loved him for that. The mother was a different can of beans, but she was pretty careful around me. I gather I missed the worst of her. She was coming down the escalator as I was going up, and she didn't dare be such a bitch any more, if she ever was as bad as they claim she was. That or she forgot what she was so pissed about.

Monica Faithful My stepson Sam came to Jimmy's wedding. He looked amazing. A full beard and big strong shoulders, all grown up. He was living in California; he'd gone out to Cal Poly after high school, and never come back east. Putting some distance between himself and Rachel, was what we thought, but maybe avoiding us too. I was surprised to see that he was close to Jimmy and Josslyn. Jimmy is always surprising you.

Josslyn Moss Jimmy's mom had no interest in my children, that's for sure. I remember once, when Virgil was a baby, we were in Dundee and we wanted to go out to dinner with another couple, friends of Jimmy's. Frannie Ober? She's in Congress. Jimmy asked his parents if we could leave Virgil with them. He was sleeping through the night and everything, I'd put him to bed myself. She said, Oh sure, even though Eleanor and Nika said she never would babysit for *them.*

We were down in the driveway when I heard Virgil screaming from the upstairs window. I mean *screaming.* I ran back up the stairs, two at a time. Mrs. Moss was holding Virgie who was red in the face, arching his back he was so upset. Maybe he felt us leaving; he is quite psychic. Anyway I took him and said to Mrs. Moss I was so sorry, I didn't think he'd wake up, and she said, "Oh, that's all right. I sort of like their little tears. I think they're kind of funny."

I thought, O-kay, lady. Get the nets . . .

Ah. Where is Sydney?

As I've said, it's hard at first to accept being dead. Much harder for some than for others. For young souls. Those with no recognition, on any level, of having been here before.

Those who have lived well and accepted much tend to slip through easily. Laurus was one of those. They look back at life and say, Well, that was great. What's next? Soon, off they go to the heavenly kaleidoscope.

Or those who have come through gradually. The very old, those who are leaving behind long illness. You've probably seen for your-self, how they drift here, then back, until finally they're so much more here than there that they stay. That's a gentle passage.

Sudden death is hard. Those who show up trailing rage and disappointments find it much harder to let go. Doesn't seem fair, does it? Well, there you go.

Monica Faithful So, the summer of sharing.

Before I answer the question, could I just say this? I *knew* what I had at stake that summer. I needed it to work, more than anyone. I knew that. But your niche in the family ecology is what it is. Your myth about how your family works is hard science, to you. It's not that easy to rebuild your emotional mousetrap just using your brain.

Eleanor Applegate Jimmy and Josslyn wanted to be at Lee-way for all of August. I mean, of course. If they're coming all the way from California, of course they'll stay a month, and August is when everyone else will be there.

Back in the fifties, when the wives used to take the children up to Maine for the whole summer, and the husbands came for a week or two when they could, it didn't matter when you were there. Now since no one but teachers can take the whole summer off, everything happens in August. So Monica wanted to be in the house all summer, and Josslyn kind of thought she should have it to herself for August if Monica had July but no one wanted to draw a line in the dirt. There were signs things weren't going to go well.

Monica Faithful Shirley Eaton called me in early June when she went to open the cottage to say the vacuum cleaner had packed up, some squirrels had been living in it. She needed to know what to do. I e-mailed everyone about it. I thought she should get a new machine from Sears. Eleanor didn't care. But Josslyn wanted to get some $700 one from Germany. Why, exactly? This is for a house that gets used two months a year!

Josslyn Moss It's ridiculous. You buy those cheap things, they're always crapping out, and up there, you're going to have to drive twenty-five miles to the repair shop, and twenty-five home, and then do it again when you pick the thing up. You buy the best, it lasts forever. I don't want to spend my vacation driving back and forth getting a crap vacuum cleaner fixed. Waste of fossil fuel. Global warming, hello? Split three ways it's only a couple hundred bucks each, anyway.

Monica Faithful Of course, I can spend hundreds of dollars on a vacuum cleaner that will be used two months a year. But I choose not to. And it's fifteen miles to Union, not twenty-five.

Jimmy Moss I called Shirley Eaton and told her I'd buy one of those German things myself and ship it to her, but she'd already gone and gotten one at Sears.

Eleanor Applegate Then there was the *Rolling Stone* situation. Charlesie had called Auggie Dodge and told him he was paying for the starboard side of the boat and the Faithfuls were paying for the port. Auggie sent Norman a bill for starting the brightwork and apparently Norman never paid it, so Auggie only did the starboard side. I guess it tickled his funny bone. But it wasn't so funny when Charlesie went up to get the boat rigged for a shakedown cruise, and found that the port side hadn't been scraped or caulked or varnished or anything. It was supposed to be a birthday present, this cruise, since he'd stayed off probation the entire spring and only had one D. We were letting him take his friends out to Roque Island.

Auggie Dodge Charlesie Applegate came in with those friends of his, their faces all full of rings and sprockets and whatnot, like they all fell down in a hardware store. He says, "Auggie, my boat's not on the mooring." And I said, "Nossir. I was all ready to put the starboard side out on the mooring when it came to me that port side had to go with it, and the port side might well fill up with water and next thing you know you'd have both sides on the bottom."

I don't know when we've had so much fun at the yard. There was that boat still in the cradle, with the starboard side all shipshape and Bristol fashion, and the port looking just like she did when we hauled her last September.

Norman Faithful I thought the bill was a joke. Monica never said a thing to me about sharing the boat.

Monica Faithful I told Norman about the boat on the way home from the lottery. I know I did. I know I did because I told him that Charlesie had wanted to take care of the boat himself and he said, God help us. And, I remember that then he talked about that time before we were married, when we sailed out to Beal Island to see the graveyard. He reached over and took my hand. I remember thinking maybe we'd go out there again and it would be nice that the boat was half ours. It's been a long time since we took a whole day and spent it alone together.

Norman Faithful If you knew what I had on my plate, you wouldn't expect a yard bill for half my wife's sailboat to be right at the top of my radar screen.

Bobby Applegate Of course, now we *do* know what he had on his plate . . .

Norman Faithful In the car going home from Cross Falls she said *something* about the *Rolling Stone* because we talked about that time we sailed to Beal Island and I heard the woman weeping. That's really why I became a priest. I don't know to this day if Nicky understands that. But I know we didn't talk about who owns the damn boat.

I believe we're surrounded by mysteries, you see. There are aspects of Christianity that are obstacles to faith, for most people. The virgin birth is one. The resurrection and ascension. The word in Koiné Greek that we translate as *virgin* means "youth." *Virgin* is a mistranslation. The resurrection? Some believe that the women outside the tomb saw Jesus' brother James. It was just a mistake, a family resemblance that let them believe in an impossible thing they longed for. How does that change the fact that Jesus was a transcendent teacher? An evolved spiritual being?

The writers of the Gospels lived in a world that thought the sky was a sort of ceiling, as if we all live in a snow globe, and that heaven was above that. They'd never flown above clouds. They had no way to measure how far away the stars are. But their world believed in mystery. They believed in faith itself, do you see? Faith for its own sake. A willingness to live with and believe in what you can't explain or understand. Faith is a muscle. The more you use it the more mysterious and powerful it grows. When I say the creeds, when I say, "I believe in the resurrection of the body and the life everlasting," I'm not saying that I personally, literally, at this moment believe that one day we'll all wake up outside the snow globe and be in our own earthly bodies again after thousands of years, and dance before the Lord. At this moment, the idea strikes me as disgusting. No, when I say the creeds I'm saying I *belong* to a church, I *belong* to a community of faith that collectively believes what the creeds say.

At present, I'll admit it, I don't understand why we believe in the resurrection of the body. But when I was six I believed I could heal people with my voice and touch. I thought I was a little vessel filled with something magic. By the time I was eight, I didn't believe any such thing. For a while the world seemed so complex, so deceptive, it seemed like a miracle that I could tie a bow and day after day it would keep my shoes on my feet.

When I was twenty, I believed that the rule of law was the way to salvation. That *laws* could be made so consistent and applied so fairly that everyone, truly, could have an equal chance to pursue happiness. I also believed I would spend the rest of my life with Rachel Cohen. What I understand now is that things change. Spirit evolves. It doesn't matter what I believe right now, it only matters that I practice faith and am willing to tolerate mystery. If I want to practice tolerating mystery by believing that Mary was a virgin and born without sin, who does it hurt?

For a long time I couldn't believe *anything* I wanted to. The law was a way to deal honorably with an uncreated universe, a world that had grown by accident. Including the accidental truth that unselfishness, and concern for our fellow men, must be an adaptive characteristic because most people seemed to prefer, innately, to be good, if you don't wreck that impulse by scorning them or starving them or depriving them of sanity and love. I thought God was a fraud, but I believed in evolution.

And then one day I heard a woman weeping whose body wasn't there.

Monica Faithful You know what my favorite season was in the Christian calendar? Lent. Forty days, most people think of as a dark wilderness time of deprivation, resisting temptation. The first Sunday in Lent is my favorite because we have the Great Litany, and all the crosses are wrapped, and there are no hallelujahs.

When we were in seminary, when most of us gave up sugar or alcohol or smoking, so we would remember Christ's time in the desert, Norman did something else. He would never talk about it; he just said that instead of giving up something, he was adding something to his practice. Those were the happiest times in our marriage. When I talked to him, he really listened. He was gentle, he was present.

I know he practiced reading the Bible in the Swedenborgian way, which he had learned from my father. You read every passage on three levels, historical, personal, and celestial. If you read about Satan taking Jesus to a high place and saying, "Go ahead, jump, let's see the angels catch you," you have to figure out what that moment was in your own life, and how you handled it.

Maybe that was it, maybe that was all. Whatever it was, he didn't go spinning off in his head and forget me. I wish I knew what it was he used to do, and whether it would help now.

Bobby Applegate The early years of our marriage, we would take Annie and Adam up to Leeway for the Fourth of July. There were fireworks at the fairgrounds that you could see all over the village, and someone always had a big family picnic. Then I'd go back down to Boston and El and the kids would stay all summer, and I'd get up when I could. We got the rooms at the back of Leeway, and Sydney and Laurus and their houseguests were up in the front rooms where you get the sun and see the water.

Monica would come for a week or two in August. Usually it took about four days before Sydney would do something to her that would have her in tears. She'd write poisonous screeds to Nika and leave them on her breakfast plate. It would be about how she had left her mug in the living room the night before instead of carrying it to the kitchen, but then zero to sixty she'd get to what a thoughtless, worthless disappointment Monica was to everyone who knew her, doomed to have a miserable life.

Here would sit the rest of us, enjoying the crackling fire and the blueberry pancakes and Sydney would be chatting away at the head of the table while Monica turned white, looking at this plateful of bile from her mother. Then Nika would leave the table and go over to Jeannie's or Amelia's for the day, and often the night, and Sydney would preen and bat her eyes at the houseguests.

Eleanor Applegate Mother couldn't seem to help herself. I think it was chemical, with her and Monica, nothing either of them could do a thing about. I know Mother tried to be good, and I believe she suffered after she'd savaged somebody but she didn't seem to remember that for long. There must have been something addictive, delicious to her, in the attack. She often denied, but she never apologized, unless she accidentally sank her fangs into someone like Bobby, who could fight back. Then she'd get terrified and be abject, which wasn't so pretty either.

Bobby put a spoke in Mother's wheels. One day one of the poison epistles appeared at Nika's place at the lunch table. Papa must not have been there. When Nika came in, Bobby said to her, "Give it here." Nika handed it across to him without reading a word. Meanwhile Big Syd sits there like lovely Mrs. Ramsay with her beef en daube in *To the Lighthouse,* dishing up Ellen's fish chowder to the Bennikes.

When Bobby finished reading the note, he got up and threw it into the fire. Then he said, "Nika, your mother wants to know if you'll be out for dinner again this evening." Nika turned and said, "I plan to be in for dinner, Mother, but if that changes I'll let you know." "Thank you very much," says Sydney, absolutely rigid. I've never loved Bobby more than at that moment. There wasn't a thing Mother could do to show how angry she was because she was giving her Gracious Hostess performance for her favorite Scandinavians.

Bobby Applegate She didn't dare attack me; she knew I could take her grandchildren and not come back. I'd rather be on the Cape with my own family anyway, and she knew it. She only really enjoyed it when she flamed someone who had to take it, her children or servants. Eleanor says she couldn't help herself, but she bloody well could; she never did it in front of Laurus, for instance.

She got me back, though. After we left she sent me a bill for all the hours Linette Gott spent on our family laundry that summer. Isn't that wonderful? The bill was huge, too. I mean, I was just getting started, both Terry and I were putting most of what we made back into the firm, and the money meant something to me. And nothing to her. Do you suppose she made Linette count the diapers and so on? When six little baby socks went into the wash and only five came out, did we still have to pay for washing the one that went missing?

Jimmy Moss Really? I don't remember Mother doing anything like that.

&

Is there marriage in Heaven? Certainly. For those to whom marriage was Heaven on earth. There is also useful work, for those who would not be themselves without it.

And sex. Yes. As I understand it.

Well, really. I'm afraid I'm just not the right one to ask about that.

&

Bobby Applegate My mother used to say that Eleanor was the daughter she always wanted. She really meant it. They used to go shopping together, have lunch and giggle. More than once I remember walking into our apartment in the evening and hearing Eleanor laughing in the kitchen. You know, the way once in a long while you laugh until you cry? I'd think, Oh, Amelia must be here, or one of El's prep school buddies, but there in the kitchen would be Eleanor and my mother. They'd both try to explain what was so funny. One time it was that my mother told El you don't want to give children bad ideas they don't already have, like don't warn them not to put beans up their nose. They couldn't even get the sentence out, they were laughing so much. No wonder Sydney couldn't stand my mother.

Eleanor Applegate Marnie Applegate really was a heavenly woman. I joined her Topics Club, and now Annie has joined, a new generation. It's a holdover from a different time for women, I know that. But it's fun. We're doing Bloomsbury this year. Annie is writing about Leonard Woolf. Somebody told her that the struggle in any marriage is over who gets to be crazy. For Leonard and Virginia it was no contest. Or for my parents, for that matter.

I'm doing Manners. I'm reading old etiquette books. Did you know that it is deeply wrong and shocking to allow your butler to wear facial hair of any kind? Emily Post, 1928 edition. Oh, I miss Marnie. She'd be loving this.

Bobby Applegate I'm sorry our youngest two never knew Mom when she was well. The good die young.

Eleanor Applegate Mother used to fuss at me for leaving my husband alone in Boston all summer. But the heat in the summer was punishing and the babies got prickly rashes and cried. And Bobby said, Don't be ridiculous. Go. It's better for you, it's better for the children. I'll be there as much as I can. It was only a five-hour drive. It was almost as if Mother *wanted* something to go wrong with my marriage.

Monica Faithful I didn't get to Dundee more than two weeks a summer, once we moved west. Often Norman didn't get there at all in those years. Eleanor and Bobby were renting the house on the Salt Pond by then, so there were years that we hardly saw each other. But when Bobby did come up, it was, Let the good times roll.

It took me a long time to see that part of the reason I married Norman was I thought he was like Bobby. Bobby likes to be happy. He likes to laugh.

Charlesie Applegate By the time we got to Dundee in the Summer of Sharing, the boatyard was flat-out and into overtime, getting the Internationals ready for the racing season. All the cruising yachts were done, except for the *Stone.* The only way I could get Auggie Dodge to have her ready before the end of July was to offer to let his father race her in the Retired Skippers' Race down in Camden, which was three weeks away.

Bobby Applegate I thought that was enterprising of Charlesie. Plus, he went down to the yard and worked on the boat himself alongside the crew, without pay.

Nora Applegate Of course, what Daddy doesn't know is that instead of the cruise they couldn't go on when the boat wasn't ready, Charlesie and his little friends "borrowed" some whalers from the yacht club and went out to Beal Island and got totally wasted. They spent the night in the graveyard and one of them saw a ghost...A horrible woman with eyes with no pupils. I know this because a couple of my friends from town were with them. They don't usually have access to such good dope.

Afterward, one of Charlesie's friends got beaten up by the guys who bring drugs in from Stonington. It never occurred to Charlesie and company that by bringing their own drugs and giving them away, they were interfering with a local economy.

Jimmy Moss The summer I was Charlesie's age, I was sent to Denmark, to work on a pig farm owned by some friends of my father's. The family was all up in Hornbæk at the beach, at least the mother and the children were. The father came and went. He had a mistress in Copenhagen, which everyone thought was normal. I was shocked.

The oldest daughter was my age, very beautiful. We had less than no interest in each other. I was in love with a girl in Dundee named Frannie Ober. Frannie gave me my first marijuana. It wasn't very good, she grew it herself, but we smoked a lot of it. In Denmark I felt as if my real life was going on in Dundee without me. Frannie was in Dundee, waiting tables at Olive's Lunch. Our whole crowd would be there together every night, and I was a world away, in a place where all it took to isolate me completely was for everyone to speak Danish. Which came pretty naturally to them.

Of course I later came to realize I'd felt most of my life that my real life must be going on somewhere else.

It was a rich farm, built around a courtyard. The house was in front, but the farm buildings were all attached to it, all the way around, so you could herd all the livestock and peasants inside and lock the gates if some neighboring baron arrived with bad intentions. Like something out of *The Seventh Seal*. When someone from the family was at home I ate with them. Otherwise I ate with the farm workers. Their favorite food was a mash made of beer and stale bread that was mixed in great vats in the farm kitchen. The pigs ate better. I've never been so bored and lonely and hungry in my life.

I rode a bike into the village to see if I could find any action, but when anyone spoke to me in Danish and I couldn't respond, they assumed I was German. They were polite; Danes are a polite people. But you don't want to be looked at like that.

I was allowed to go down to Fyn to my grandparents' beach cottage only once. Not that that was so lively, but there were pretty girls in tiny bathing suits on the beach there, some topless. We didn't get a lot of that in Dundee, Maine. My only other escape was to go into Copenhagen to stay with Aunt Nina. The first time, she drove up in her little deux chevaux to get me. I still remember driving out of that courtyard with her, while the rest of the men were finishing up the Friday chores. If I'd spoken Danish I believe my sentiments would have been, So long, suckers.

Aunt Nina took me to concerts, and to jazz clubs in the city. She tried to get me to play the piano, which no one had in a long time, but I looked at those keys and felt they would burn my fingers if I touched them. The keyboard seemed to pulse. It had a sick glow, and could expand and contract.

Honestly, that last is probably a vision from later. But it was Nina's keyboard I was seeing. Later in the summer Aunt Nina went to France and left me the keys to her apartment. I spent a weekend there, part of the time with some Spanish girls I'd met at Tivoli Gardens, and one of them left a long black cigarette burn on the kitchen table. The table was new. I never mentioned it to Nina, and she never mentioned it to me.

My world was tiny. It was the size of my head. What

was real was what I personally could see or feel and what I felt was: Alienated. Everywhere. It was excruciating.

Benedikte Bastlund I remember an American Moss boy at the farm one summer. Interesting looking, but sullen, and with no curiosity or languages. He had no idea that his sister Monica was named for a hero of our Resistance. He didn't even know that his aunt had been in a concentration camp during the war. She was a marvelous woman, Nina Moss. But the American nephew, Johnny, was not of interest. I really can't remember much about him except how much he complained about our tobacco. If you don't like it, don't smoke, for heaven's sake.

Frannie Ober Oh well, you know. First love. My parents didn't much want me hanging out with rich summer kids, so that made him very attractive. He was furious at his father and I was furious at my mother, always a bond. I don't know why I was furious. I think maybe it was that my mother and I had been too close when I was growing up and I didn't know how to draw away gradually. I was too important to her, you know? For her own reasons, which weren't my reasons. But why was Jimmy so mad at his father? I don't remember. Really, he was mad at everybody. He said he was a cuckoo in the wrong nest.

There was a time when we thought we would run away together and live on Beal Island, and make all our clothes and food ourselves. It was the sixties. We'd have windmills to make electricity. I'd weave cloth and make patchwork quilts. Jimmy was going to fish and farm and we'd raise beautiful barefoot babies, a girl for him and a boy for me, and we'd never misunderstand them and they'd be perfect humans. Doesn't it sound wonderful?

For one thing, Jimmy was very, very funny, especially when he was drunk or stoned. He was mean, but he was funny. Mean about other people, his parents and sisters, never mean to me that first summer. And of course there was sex, which we personally invented. I'm surprised you didn't know that.

But the second summer, when he came back from Denmark, he was different. He was or I was. He was more angry than funny. Once or twice he turned that on me, and I didn't like it. Plus I was going to college in the fall and looking forward to it. Jimmy wasn't looking forward to anything.

He hitchhiked to visit me in Northampton that winter and brought a couple of tabs of LSD. I don't know where he got it. He was supposed to be finishing high school but it sounded as if all he did was hang around Harvard Square. He got angry that I wouldn't drop acid with him, and I told him I didn't want to see him any more.

Jimmy Moss I was completely lost when Frannie broke up with me. She was my world, she was all I could see. I wanted to kill her. I thought she'd taken my life from me.

I hung around the music scene in Cambridge. You could live for nothing in those days, and I did. We were all going to live together and die together, *mi casa es su casa,* the musicians. The freaks. There was a lot of dope, and we discovered macrobiotics; *that* was going to change the world. We had malnutrition and we weren't very clean, but the highs were something. There was plenty of acid if you knew the right people. There was a whole apartment down in Kinnaird Street painted black, an acid factory. You could crash there too.

God, it's weird to speak this language again. Another country and another time.

I met a guy who'd spent a summer in Peru and brought back a gourd full of coca powder that he'd learned about from the Quechua people. They were the last of the Incas. Wait, maybe it was coca leaves, and you'd chew them and then activate the drug by dipping a wire into the powder in the gourd and licking it. I forget.

There were magic mushrooms. There were peyote buttons. I'd try anything. And I threw up a lot.

The music scene. The Jug Band—people making music by blowing across the top of a jug? Playing washtub bass? Playing the washboard with thimbles? Bluegrass on fiddles, blues on a twelve-string guitar—it was like LSD, when the rocks and trees start talking to you. Those instruments made out of nothing, that lost music, suddenly pouring out of every open window. For other people, maybe the music was one diversion among others. For me, it was like the music breathed for me.

When I worked, I worked as a roadie. I'd carry those people's amps, I'd drive their third-hand vans, just to be welcome in the dressing rooms. The one thing I wouldn't do was work for a band that used keyboards. That was too dangerous. It would be like being taken up to the top of a steeple and dared to jump off to prove I could fly. Way too dangerous. For who I was then.

On my first LSD trip, I walked around Cambridge Common with some boy who'd taken what, two trips? So he was my "guide." On the grass in the sun I saw a little girl in an orange coat and realized she was God. It was all so clear. I wanted Frannie to see God too, with me. I wanted her to be unhooked from all the things that link you to your tribe, all their programming, then we'd be free together.

Frannie Ober I hadn't wanted to break up with Jimmy that weekend. But he got so hurt and angry. He said I didn't understand what I was saying no to. I said I just couldn't give away an entire weekend, I had papers to write. Also, I'd heard from someone that acid could cause chromosome damage that would hurt your babies. That made him madder—that I would give some wild rumor about something that might damage some imaginary baby ten years from now more power than going to find God with him right then. We were on completely different tracks. I told him I loved him and I hoped that he'd come back to me someday, but for right then, I wanted him to go away.

I can't tell you how many times I wanted to call him back to me. But who knew how to reach him? And he was so proud, I knew he'd never call me. It was a miserable winter. Sometimes I'd hear rumors about him. Angry, funny, beautiful, trapped Jimmy. I'm not sure that I don't still miss him. A couple of years later I even tried LSD with some other guy. I saw a lot of colors I'd never seen before, or thought I hadn't. I spent about four hours looking at an artichoke. But I guess to see God, I'd have had to trip with Jimmy. And he was long gone.

Jimmy Moss Once Monica came to Cambridge to find me. She bought me dinner and gave me all her money. I explained about how I lived, and that I was all right. I told her I'd heard the Carter Family play in the basement of a church right off the Square. Mother Maybelle Carter herself with her auto-harp. Monica got it. She told me Mom was wild when I didn't come home for Christmas. I said to tell her Too bad.

Monica Faithful I went to find him because I missed him, but also because I knew Mother had cut off his allowance, thinking that would force him home. I didn't want it to drive him further away, where we *couldn't* find him. He showed me where he was living at the time. I met a couple of his friends. He was very thin and had a scraggy armpit beard, but he seemed sane. He let me buy him a steak, even though he said his girlfriend wouldn't come near him when he ate meat, she said the smell came out on his skin. I asked him to tell me more about her and he said, "Well, she hasn't given me crabs yet."

Jimmy Moss Nika gave me her number at college and I called her now and then. Just to hear her voice, or some-times to ask for money, which she always sent if she had it. But I didn't go home for a couple of years, and when I did, it was to ask them to give me my share of what would come to us when they died. Papa understood what I was saying. I wanted them to be dead to me.

I did also want the money. I'd met some people who'd gone in search of living shamans. Some musician friends who mostly did weed were getting paranoid behind it. The acid thing, with no real guides, could be just another light show. Or it could turn dark. I don't mean the famous flash-backs, or the kids who thought they could walk on water and drowned instead. I mean that if the rocks and trees start talking to you and you don't know which ones to listen to, you can go down a shadow path. I'd seen God once and I wanted more of the real thing. The drugs by themselves weren't showing me anything new.

These days, I see my father every time I look in the mirror. It's a comfort. My hands are his hands. I catch sight of myself in a glass from the corner of my eye, and there he is. It always makes me happy.

But then? I was enraged at him for not protecting me. From being smothered, from being used as a stand-in for some perfect being my mother thought she loved. Not that I understood any of that. I wanted Jimmy Moss to dry up and split open like an old pod and let some new being emerge pink and naked, a child of the universe instead of a particular human family. Every family is a story. Every single one. But I was sick of mine. Or maybe of all of them.

I don't really know where the inheritance went. I wasn't exactly keeping meticulous records. Most of the time I couldn't keep track of my socks. I left Cambridge. And wound up guess where, San Francisco. The freaks there were more serious about their spirit lives, but they also had some meaner dope. Cocaine. Junk. I saw some things that really, really scared me, which wasn't all bad. I heard of some stuff called ibogaine made from bark in Africa, that gives you a different kind of trance, where you see your whole past and understand it. I decided to go there. I wanted to take it with the people who discovered it, in the birthplace of *Homo sapiens*. That required a major amount of dealing with the institutional universe. Money, passports, visas. Airplane tickets. (I took a few people with me.)

A year or two after that, I decided to do ayahuasca, from the Amazon, in the Amazon. I took a few people with me that time too. Two of the women had their moons when we finally got where we were going and weren't allowed to be part of the ceremony. One of the guys just pissed himself and vomited the whole time, which was disappointing for him. I got where I was going, though. That's when I began making my way back.

Monica Faithful I thought it would be easy to share the house. That's really what I thought. It was going to be great for everybody. Dundee was my life on an ideal planet. In Connecticut when I was young, people noticed if my hair was all wrong, and that I had no backhand and didn't care. In the places Norman and I had lived, I was always having to present myself and explain myself, to try to guess what was expected and then live up to it. In Dundee, it was as if I had twenty brothers and sisters who all saw the point of me, and I of them. We'd sailed together, fallen in and out of love when we were teenagers, our parents were friends and our children are friends. My friends there read books and play cellos. Some of them are eighty, some of them are ten. It's the place where I always feel that I belong. Some people never feel that anywhere.

So I had planned to get up to Dundee early and I could have helped get the boat straightened out, but to be frank, things in Sweetwater were feeling very...I don't know, itchy. I was distracted. Norman's new curate was a woman named Lindsay Tautsch. She's one of those square-shaped young women, stolid, like an engineer, and she runs rather cool. At least with me. Also, she'd grown up in the area and had her own little power base. In early June, she suggested we have lunch together. It wasn't convenient for me, but we had it, and I couldn't figure out why. I kept waiting for her to drop her bomb or ask her question . . . let me know what the subtext was. She never did. We ate our soup and half a sandwich, and then I ordered coffee and she ordered hot water, and she looked at me kindly, and sighed.

Norman Faithful I came home between counseling appointments to hear what La Tautsch had wanted, and Nicky wasn't there. She was downtown buying more books. This is a sickness. She had about eleven books in a stack by her nest in the den that she hadn't finished or even started, and here were three more, one a great fat book about Vichy France that cost thirty-five dollars! If she lived to be 108 she'd never get to read them all.

Monica Faithful Then one of my favorite people in the parish, old Mr. Sector who'd been an elder for decades, got crosswise with Norman because he kept singing the old tunes to the hymns when Norman had called for the new improved ones. Norman is all about the church keeping up with the times. Change is good. Mr. Sector couldn't carry a tune in a bucket so it didn't make much difference what tune he sang, but as senior warden he leads a lot of people in the community so Norman called him on the carpet about it. Mr. Sector told his wife he'd been called down to the church to be exorcised.

He always wore a cutaway and a top hat on Easter Sunday, Mr. Sector. They're lovely people.

Norman took the job at Good Shepherd in Sweetwater

about a year after the Hawaii business. He needed a fresh start, and he thought the parish might be a better fit for him than New York had been. But things haven't always been smooth sailing for us in Sweetwater either. For starters, on his very first Sunday Norman looked out on the congregation and there in the third row sat the McChesneys, his tormentors from Holy Innocents. They'd driven all the way across the state of Pennsylvania to be there and go to the coffee hour and stir up trouble. Do you believe it?

Norman weathered that, but he did then get out in front of his constituents in a couple of ways. He took a stand in favor of gay marriage that he could have prepared them for better than he did, and he published a pamphlet called *A Priest Asks,* about the spirit world. Why, he asks, if we believe that Jesus' spirit was personally intact after the death of his body, so that he could appear to people and everything, wouldn't we also believe that something similar happens to the rest of us? If Jesus' life is a pattern for us to follow? Of course, some people found it threatening, and some found it plain nuts. Then a couple of years after we got there, Norman went off campaigning to be bishop of New Jersey. It was Hawaii all over again. He made the final cut, he was by far the best preacher, and he had great strengths the diocese needed, but it went to the archdeacon of the diocese. Another inside candidate. Norman took it hard. Really hard. And people in the parish didn't like thinking that Norman saw Good Shepherd as a booby prize. Why should they? They think Sweetwater is paradise.

Norman Faithful Her nest is new, since the family lottery. She's got this old chair that was her father's. It needs recovering so she had some grisly quilt draped over it and somehow she's shaping it so it kind of fills in around her when she climbs into it. I'm pretty sure she hops in there to build it with twigs and scraps of bunny tail fluff in her beak.

Rebecca Vogelsang Of course I've only been in Sweetwater a few years. But Good Shepherd has been my church home from the first. Father Faithful is a gifted preacher and a gifted counselor. He worked with me and Clark when we first got here. We had stretched to buy a house on the Heights with a lawn and a pool when Clark was moved here, and then he got fired. It was a bad time. Father Faithful didn't just comfort and pray with us, he got involved. He'd call Clark up and say, "I was thinking about you, let's have lunch." I started teaching Sunday school and Clark eventually went on the vestry.

We might have moved back to Cincinnati if it hadn't been for Norman, even though the children were settled in school and we loved the community. Norman kept saying if we prayed and trusted the Lord, Clark would get another job, and of course he did.

It's true, Norman can be erratic. He's not one to lead meditation hikes or go on prayer retreats, and sometimes he moves too fast. He lives in the world; he gives a hundred percent to the Here and Now. There are plenty of us broken and needing healing walking around the A&P, it doesn't take a pilgrimage to find us. Probably he gets too involved. Maybe he acts before he's thought everything through. But he was a lifesaver for us.

When I heard that Lindsay Tautsch was going around in her vestments saying, "You know, I always have a sermon ready in my pocket in case Father Faithful can't perform," it made me very angry.

Calvin Sector Of course Norman Faithful's been known to take a drink. So have I. So have you. I mean it's an old joke: where two or three Episcoplians are gathered in His name, there's bound to be a fifth. There's no need to hold the man to an inhuman standard. He's not supposed to *be* Jesus Christ. Who liked his wine as well as the next man, by the by.

Monica Faithful I left for Dundee the very end of June. Sweetwater was lovely, lush and green. The back fence at the rectory is covered in honeysuckle, and when it blooms it fills the air with scent and the neighborhood children come over to pull the stems out of the blossoms backward to get that pure drop of nectar on their tongues. Of course the bees are busy; I love the sound of them. And the beech and oak and maple trees on our street form great green vaulted ceilings above our heads. But it does get horribly hot, and we only have air-conditioning in our bedroom. The church is cool, of course.

Rebecca Vogelsang And keep in mind, all last winter Norman had the worry of moving his mother to a nursing home. She broke her hip and they thought that would kill her but it didn't. But she couldn't live alone after that. She couldn't keep her pills straight or remember if she'd eaten. Norman was brought to tears when he talked about it. He's an only child, he had to do it all himself. Well, of course, Nicky helped when she wasn't too busy with her own family.

Norman found a very nice place for Mrs. F., and Norman was paying for it all. Three weeks after they moved her in, the place called up and said they couldn't keep her, she had too much dementia and they weren't equipped for it. He had to go all through it again. Find a new place, who knows how many trips back and forth. The new one is the kind of place where you have to give them all your assets and you never get them back. Not that she has much, so Norman had to take care of that too. It was terribly hard on him. And Monica just left him. Off she went to Maine to spend the summer with her people.

Monica Faithful When I got to Leeway Cottage, I walked into the front bedroom with my suitcases and a half-naked girl walked out of the bathroom. She was obviously living there. She looked startled to see me.

Alison Boyd I was plenty surprised, standing in my undies. I said, "May I help you?"

Monica Faithful I said, "I'm Monica Moss. This is my house. And you are . . . ?"

A summer or two ago, when my parents arrived, they found clear signs that someone had been living in the back of the house. A bed was unmade and there was a big gruntie floating in the toilet. I thought, My heavens, this one has some crust, moving right into the best guest room.

Alison Boyd I said, "OH! Aunt Monica . . . no one knew when you were arriving. I'm Alison, Adam's friend."

Monica Faithful I was nonplussed. Shirley certainly knew when I was coming, and I said so.

Alison Boyd I hadn't seen Shirley yet. Eleanor and Bobby hadn't seemed to know, and since they suddenly had a full house, they told us to go to Leeway. We had just gotten there the night before.

Monica went straight to the phone.

Eleanor Applegate I said, "Ohmigod, are you here? I spoke to Norman three days ago and he said he didn't know when you were leaving. Didn't he tell you?"

Monica Faithful Of course he didn't tell me, when had she ever known Norman to give me a message? Eleanor said that Adam and Alison came early as a surprise and she still had a coven of houseguests, and did I mind terribly? I didn't, but was I supposed to let them share a bedroom? She said, "Well, they do live together in Washington," and I said that didn't answer my question, and she said, "Then do whatever Mother would have done, isn't that the rule for Leeway this summer?" So I told this girl she should move into Mother and Papa's bedroom since it would creep *me* out to sleep there, and I would take the big guest room, which she'd been in, and Adam could sleep across the hall. I went down to the kitchen where Shirley was having a high old time feeding Adam blueberry pancakes. I sent her up to change the sheets for me in "my" bedroom. Of course I spent the rest of the week bumping into one or the other at midnight or the crack of dawn, creeping back and forth across the hall.

Adam Applegate The next thing that happened was, Nika noticed the grandparents' ashes weren't on the mantelpiece where they had been left last fall. Housewide crisis. Shirley said she hadn't touched them. I asked Marlon, the caretaker— he's a little slow, and he remembered taking some old tins to the dump but he couldn't describe them. Nika was in a state.

Monica Faithful I rushed into El's house, a wreck, to tell her we'd lost the ashes, when I saw the urns on her mantel-piece. I said, "Why didn't you tell me you took those?"

Eleanor Applegate Yelled is more like it.

Monica Faithful And she said, "Because you just walked in the door!" And that was true. So I calmed down and said I was sorry and she said she was too, but it wasn't ... You know, it wasn't a very nice way to begin the summer. Not even counting the "who's been sleeping in my bed" issue. I felt like an hysteric. Ugh.

Once I got to know her, I liked Alison very much. She had a lovely sense of humor. She seemed a little lost, in want of mothering; her own mother was dead. We had some delightful talks on the porch while Adam was off playing golf with his childhood buddies. Dundee can be a bit much when you're new. There's a limit to how many times you want to hear the story about the time Colin Gantry threw up in the wastebasket, or the time Gordon Maitland, racing his ketch in a gale, handed his houseguest the steering wheel, which he'd secretly unscrewed, and said, "You take the helm, I'm going below."

I was sorry when Adam and Alison moved back over to the Salt Pond.

Eleanor Applegate When my houseguests finally left, we had a dinner for Adam and Alison. I was hoping they might announce their engagement. The party kept growing, though, as it turned out more of Adam's friends were in town and then suddenly Edie and Sylvie showed up for the weekend, Sylvie with a beau. At that point, we decided to move the whole feast to Leeway, where the table can expand to seat something huge, twenty people or so. Nika and I did all the cooking and the kids helped with everything—duh, half of them are professional food people. Edie is going to chef school. Even Bobby helped.

Monica Faithful I was afraid it would feel haunted to have a dinner party in Mother and Papa's house without them, but you know what? It was great. It felt as if we were finally grown-ups ourselves. What are we, in our fifties? I liked Sylvie's beau, Edie made fabulous tartes tatin, and Alison was adorable. She was working hard to keep straight which of the friends were cousins, and who had had summer romances . . . you could see her falling in love with it, the Brigadoon effect.

After dinner, when the table was cleared, we played UpJenkins. Mother and Papa's happy spirits were hovering.

BETH GUTCHEON

They were back on the Leeway mantelpiece; Eleanor brought them with her; she said they hadn't wanted to miss the season opener.

At that point Alison was beside me and I noticed she was wearing a very striking ring, a huge amethyst in an old-fashioned setting with little pearls. She took it off and showed it to me. It had been her mother's.

In the middle of the night, I got it, why I couldn't get over that ring. Patsy Starr had had a ring exactly like that when we were in boarding school. I'd been fascinated by the way the stone changed color in different lights. It could look blue or purple or even green. I'd never seen an amethyst before. We weren't supposed to bring valuable things to school, plus I was surprised at someone our age having it at all.

I hadn't seen Patsy in donkey's years, so the next day I called the alumnae office and got her number. We had a great catch-up. Finally I said, "Patsy, remember that antique ring you had when we were in school?" She said it was made for her grandmother, and why did I ask? I told her, my nephew's girl blah blah, and there was a long silence. I was thinking, is Alison related to her somehow?

Finally she said, "When I was first married, I was at a dinner party in New York. We got to talking about the jewelry at the table, where our pieces came from, what the family stories were. Someone suggested we pass them around, so we did. And when that was over, my ring had disappeared."

I couldn't speak for a moment. Way creepy. I asked the obvious question.

She said, "What *could* I do? I couldn't ruin the party. I told my hostess as I was leaving. We went back to the dining room and crawled around on the floor; it wasn't there. She put her staff on the watch for it, you know, they cut open the vacuum cleaner bags the next day and so forth, but it never turned up."

Patsy asked me the name of Alison's mother. I told her. And was she at the dinner party? She was. They were friends. Patsy went to her funeral.

I asked her what she wanted me to do. She said, "Tell Alison her mother had beautiful taste."

Norman Faithful We tried to have a phone call every couple of days once Nicky left for Dundee, but it was hard. By the time she got in from some dinner party, I was often in bed. Naturally, I went down to visit Mother whenever I could. Things weren't cooling down at all this July. The minister over at the United Presby Church is a sort of cult leader in a cassock. They have people coming in buses from Ohio and West Virginia to his services. He does a huge nine o'clock and eleven o'clock on Sundays, plus there are youth services, there are sing-alongs, even a Friday evening Speaking in Tongues. They'd bought a house next door to the church and torn it down to make room for more parking. The family that sold them the house was irate, and the village wasn't well pleased either, that the lot was removed from the tax rolls. It wasn't as if these busloads of born-again Protestants were spending money in town.

Naturally a lot of the Presby old guard were coming over to worship with us, but that was not an unmixed blessing. They weren't used to common chalice communion; they were upset that we have two side aisles in the nave instead of a center aisle. Brides don't like it. I had deputations of new members coming to get me to tear out our pews. One family whose daughter is getting married this fall even offered to pay for it. The minute word of that gets out, deputations of *old* members would arrive to tell me their grandparents would spin in their graves...I saw a hole in my schedule, and decided I could take a weekend and get out of Dodge.

Monica Faithful It was perfect. Norman told me on a Wednesday he would be there Friday night. The weather was gorgeous and likely to stay that way all weekend. Nora was living at Leeway because she was working on the famous family archive in the living room, on the big table where we usually did jigsaw puzzles. I didn't want to tell her to clear out for the weekend, it would have embarrassed us both. You don't want your beloved niece to picture you and the rector chasing each other naked through the bedrooms or Auntie Nika serving him breakfast in bed dressed like Fifi the French maid. Neither scenario was very likely, by the way, but we needed some alone time together, we really did. And the *Rolling Stone* was on her mooring as of that morning.

I decided to surprise Norman and take him out for an overnight. We could spend the day on Beal Island, explore the old foundations, whatever he wanted, and then sail down to Loon Island. There is nothing in the world, nothing, like being at anchor in a wild cove, with only the light and the gulls and the rocking of the boat on the water to fill your senses.

I planned the menus for two days. I drove to Union for supplies. I made egg salad and gazpacho and went to a special store for Norman's favorite kind of beer, and got out the coolers and pillows and linens for the double bunk. I went down to the yacht club to bring the boat to the dock for water and ice and gas, and it was gone.

Syl Conary Mrs. Faithful came up to the manager's shack. She looked a little druv up, but she was perfectly polite. An angel from heaven compared to her mother. She says, "Syl, where is the *Rolling Stone*?" And I say, "Camden by now, I expect." And she says, "Camden?" And I says, "Charlesie Applegate took her down this morning so Mutt Dodge can race her in the Retired Skippers' tomorrow." "I see," she says. And after a while, she says Mutt Dodge was a great friend of her father's and he'd be pleased. I told her I hope it wasn't a problem and she said no, of course not, she was just surprised.

Eleanor Applegate We were playing bridge with Lincoln and Janet Cluett Saturday night when Charlesie, Jeff Pease, and Auggie and Mutt Dodge walked in. They were still in their sailing clothes and Mutt was holding a trophy. Well, I just screamed.

Lincoln Cluett We all crowded around them. I said, "You won? You won the Retired Skippers' Race in a wooden boat?" Mutt looked so lit up I thought he might levitate. "I lay it all to my tactician," he said, meaning Charlesie.

Charlesie Applegate You should have seen it! The breeze died after we rounded the windward mark. Of course the plastic boats were all way ahead of us and we saw their chutes go flat one after another—they had sailed right into a hole. Mutt had me up on the bow with glasses scanning for wind. We still had some way on, which the leaders didn't. I could see there was some texture on the water over on the other side of Egg Rock, so we made for that.

Eleanor Applegate Mutt said, "We went spooking past the fleet while they lay becalmed. By the time they finally got some air back, we were around the leeward mark, doing eight knots to windward and we could see the finish line." That's a lo-o-ong speech for him, but he was grinning to beat the band.

Bobby Applegate There were high fives all around, and El went out to the kitchen to heat up some dinner for them. Mutt and Auggie said they just came to drop Charlesie off, they had to get Jeff home and go tell their wives, but we made them stay for a glass of champagne. What pleased me as much as anything was seeing the new respect Mutt and Auggie had for Charlesie. Big difference from the way the summer started.

Eleanor Applegate All I could think was how thrilled Papa would have been. I know Mutt was thinking it too, but neither of us said a word about it. He tried to give the trophy to me. "Now El," he said, "it's your boat, I was just the nut holding the tiller." Bobby said, "Mutt, it's called the Retired *Skippers'* Race." "Well, if you're sure," he said, "the wife will be some tickled." And they went off. How old is Mutt, I wonder? Got to be late eighties . . .

We gave up cards and sat around the dining room table

while Charlesie ate and told us the whole story again, from starting gun to the look on the faces of the fleet hotshots as the old *Stone* went by them.

Then Charlesie went to shower and get ready to go out and find his friends. We finally finished our rubber, and the Cluetts went home. Charlesie came down and we sent him off into the night to howl, except two minutes later he was back inside, looking as if someone had punched him. All the wind was knocked right out of his sails. You know they say you're only as happy as your unhappiest child? When Charlesie gets knocked down he gets *so* down, and it takes him so long to climb out of it, it tears the heart right out of me.

So that was the end of that happy evening.

Bobby Applegate He'd found a letter in his car. From Monica.

How *could* she? I mean, really.

Eleanor Applegate He wouldn't show it to us. He said it wasn't that bad, it was only she was mad he hadn't told her he had plans for the boat, since she's half owner. Charlesie was upset because he knew he should have told her, but he hadn't thought of it and certainly no one else had either. The boat wouldn't be in the water at all if it weren't for Charlesie, and whose fault was it that it was late? Plus, it had been years since she'd taken that boat anywhere by herself, *none* of us had thought she might want it. I felt terrible for Charlesie, and frankly I was furious at Monica.

Bobby Applegate I said to El, "Don't even think about talking to your sister about this. If either of you says things you shouldn't, we'll be years getting over it." Mostly I wanted my wife to calm down enough to sleep or we'd all have hell to pay. I told her to go sit and read a book and I'd build her a fire and bring her some tea, and tomorrow I'd talk to Monica myself.

Eleanor Applegate After a while Charlesie came down-stairs again, said he felt better and was going out after all, so I began to settle down. But when someone takes your child's joy away, don't you just want to rip their throats out?

Bobby Applegate Nora told us Monica and Norman had gone hiking on Mount Desert and spent the night at the Asticou. The next day I was waiting for her at Leeway when she came back from driving Norman to the afternoon plane. She puttered in and out for a while, hanging things up, looking for some keys, offering me things to eat and drink. I asked how her weekend had gone, and she said it would have been better if she'd been able to get Norman out of range of where his cell phone worked. I wasn't hav-ing any of that.

I waited her out and she finally came and sat down. We sat for a little bit. I wanted her to figure out for herself why I was there, though really I think she knew it the minute she saw me.

I said, "Monica, when you're upset with one of our children, don't you think you should come to us before you light their hair on fire?" She showed me her poker face. She said, "If you had something to say to Edith, I'd expect you to say it to her. It was between me and Charlesie."

I said, "First thing: What upsets our children upsets all of us, very much, so it wasn't just between the two of you. Second thing: Edith is a young adult, and I still don't believe you'd like it one bit if I ripped her up and down, even if she deserved it. And Charlesie is still a teenager. He's having enough trouble growing up, without the people who are supposed to love him knocking the pins out from under him."

She asked if he showed us the letter. I said, "No, he wouldn't. I think he was trying to protect *you*, by the way. And he said it wasn't that bad, but we have to go by how much your anger upset him. Which was very much."

She said, "I wasn't angry! I was very disappointed!"

I said, "And now you're all over it and he feels like hammered shit. Why didn't you *talk* to him instead of leaving him a letter?" She said he was already gone when she went to see him. I asked why she didn't wait till he got back, and she said because she was upset. And I said, "A letter, Monica? Sitting on the seat of his car like a poison toad waiting for him, while you're all over your snit and on to the next thing? From you, of all people?"

She didn't look very happy. Finally she said, "And what do you expect me to do?" I said, "I hope you'll apologize to him." She said, "I don't know if I can." So I went home.

Eleanor Applegate By the way—had she told Charlesie that *she* planned to use the boat? I don't remember taking *that* message . . .

Monica Faithful I had a horrible night. Nora settled in after supper to work on her archive. She told me about Mutt winning the Retired Skippers', and how excited and proud everyone was of Charlesie, so I got the picture pretty good of what I'd done. I really can't talk about it.

Charlesie Applegate Aunt Nika was waiting for me at the yacht club when I came in from the *Stone* the next afternoon. She said she was very sorry about the letter, and I said, no, like, she was right, I should have told her, and I was embarrassed. She said she was proud of us that we won, and how happy Grandpapa would be if he was watching from his cloud, yada yada. I mean, he would, I know. Then she asked if it would be fun if she and Nora and I planned a surprise birthday party for Mom? Like, would I help her? Mom would be really surprised; since she was turning fifty-eight, she wouldn't think anything special was coming. I said cool with me if Nora's up for it.

Monica Faithful That gave us two and a half weeks. We would do it at Leeway, of course. Bobby looked thoughtful about it, but he said he was in. He'd keep El on the water all day, and tell her he was taking her down to the Gray Goose Inn for dinner. I put Charlesie in charge of finding a band, and Nora on decorations. I hired a caterer. I called Cinder and Marta, her best friends since boarding school, and they promised to come. Marta had to come from France. I even got Rufus Maitland to stay, although he was due to leave for Islamabad that week. Rufus was Eleanor's first love. He's never married, in spite of being approximately the handsomest man you ever saw. He speaks eight languages, that I know of. He's always off for years, living in trouble spots, where he pretends he sells farm equipment, and we pretend we believe him.

Josslyn Moss Nika *did* call us in California and ask if she could give this birthday party in August at Leeway, and Jimmy was all for it. Why shouldn't he be? *He* wasn't going to have to change the sheets or bake the cake. But I pictured maybe a dinner party, not a fucking bar mitzvah. Also, I assumed Monica would move to the back of the house when we got there, since she'd had the front for a month. But no. She seemed totally surprised at the thought. She was settled in the best guest room, and Norman was coming, and he preferred the front rooms because the ceilings were higher and he's tall. Please.

I said we'd take Sydney and Laurus's room, and she said, Fine, but Jimmy didn't want to be out of earshot of the kids. I said they could all sleep in the room across the hall, and he said, No, we'd just gotten Boedie to sleep in her own bed, if we put her in with her brothers she'd end up back in bed with us. So we took the rooms in the back. Again.

Monica Faithful Boedie had an earache when the young Mosses got here, and was very whiny. I offered to move to the back rooms but Jimmy said there was no need, that Boedie would sleep better in rooms that didn't get morning sun and they wanted to be close to her in case she needed them at night. Adam and Alison were coming back to surprise Eleanor, hiding out with me until the night of the party, so that was just as well, they could have their same rooms back.

The Leeway Cottage Guestbook *August 2, 1999. Arrived after a long trip, tired but happy to be here. Shirley had left chicken pie and blueberry muffins for supper and the children roasted marshmallows in the fireplace for dessert. Everyone had hot baths except Boedie; Virgil had convinced her that the bathtubs were alive, because of their claw feet. Joss bathed her in the kitchen sink. Nika and I sat out on the porch watching the stars until all hours (still on California time). There are so many here, compared to L.A. J. Moss*

Jimmy Moss Frankly I'd forgotten about the party. The great drama in our lives was a puppy we had promised the children. They wanted a Dalmatian, because of that movie, and I said no. They're not good with children and they need much too much exercise. They wanted to get it last Christ-mas but I said no, because Josslyn has never had a dog, and I didn't have time to housetrain it right then. So for six months, we've been planning for our August puppy. Off we went to Orono where a lady we found on the Internet had a litter of yellow Labs ready to go. The minute I saw them I knew the father was no Lab. Their paws were enormous. I hoped the other half wasn't Newfy or wolf. By the time your children have puppies in their arms, though, the ship has sailed. At that point, the battle was limiting them to one. Regis chose him, Boedie named him Toto, and Virgil is the one he threw up on on the way home.

Virgil Applegate It was green with lumps. Mom and Boedie were grossed out. Daddy said all puppies get carsick and he'd grow out of it.

Monica Faithful I'm pretty sure Jimmy told me about the puppy. He says he e-mailed me. It must have seemed like a good idea at the time. Puppies are like childbirth, you can't remember how awful it is until it's too late. And it always lasts about a month longer than you can stand it. Oh well—not my problem.

Marta Rowland It's a nightmare, getting to Dundee. I decided to fly to Portland and rent a car. You still have a three-hour drive after that, and I was on Paris time, but the last time I flew to Bangor, Charlesie picked me up and drove me out to the coast at nine hundred miles an hour. I was in fear for my life.

Monica had e-mailed directions to me but no one ever thought I'd missed a career as a pathfinder. I saw a good deal of scenic Vacationland before I got to Janet Cluett's house. Cinder and her husband were already there when I finally found them, and we had quite a house party. We had to stay away from any place we might run into Eleanor, so if we went downtown or out on the water, we wore huge hats and sunglasses. It was rather fun. We felt like Mata Hari.

Josslyn Moss The puppy had to live in the kitchen when he wasn't being constantly watched, as we were still in the paper-training stage. Also, he chewed. We sprayed all chair legs with Bitter Apple but Toto seemed to love it. Jimmy asked Adam and Alison if they had any food in their rooms, and if they did, would they please give it to him so he could put it where the puppy wouldn't get it. Alison had a fancy tin of shortbread in her suitcase she was taking to her next hostess after she left us and she was embarrassed to mention it. The puppy got right through the tin, and afterward ate a whole bag of her cotton balls too. Then he was spectacularly sick on the carpet in the hall.

A houseful of people I barely know when I'm trying to raise a family and a puppy. This is a vacation?

Monica Faithful Mother's dining room chairs have all got gnaw marks now. There are two armchairs and ten side chairs that Annabelle Brant bought in England. I mean we weren't going to sell them but people who know antiques say they're rather special. I knew Eleanor would mind, when she saw them. Meanwhile it was all I could do to keep her out of the house, where the furniture had been moved for dancing, and Nora was stringing balloons.

Norman arrived the day before the birthday and I made him take El out to play golf. You know the story about the young couple who can't afford a fancy roast when the boss comes to dinner so they decide she'll come out of the kitchen and say, "Oh dear, the roast fell on the floor," and then the husband will say, "Never mind, we'll have the stuffed cabbage." But instead she comes out and says, "Oh dear, the stuffed cabbage fell on the floor," and he says, "You mean the roast," but she doesn't. Our excuse was like that. Norman was going to tell her that I'd join them, and then when I was late I'd say that I'd had to take the puppy to the vet. Boy, did I. The caterers let him out of the kitchen when they came to put things into the icebox. By the time I found him he'd more or less eaten one of Norman's Gucci loafers. Fortunately when I showed up to walk the last hole with them and told him I'd had to take the puppy to the vet, he still thought it was the stuffed cabbage story.

Norman Faithful I mean it was a zoo. Edie was there but Sam and Sylvie weren't. I suppose no one invited them. And then Jimmy's frigging dog ate my shoe and the only other ones I had were ancient clam diggers that I leave in the house over the winter. I looked ridiculous, and do you have an idea how much those shoes cost? I had to drive to Union to buy a pair of clodhoppers. Which I'll probably never wear again.

I've been brushing up my Koiné to read the Gospels in the original, and I'm struck by how often our Lord warns us against overidentifying with tribe or family of origin. He says that if you don't hate your mother and father you cannot follow Him. All these Family Values preachers just think, Well, He can't have really meant that. But He did. He meant that clinging to your tribe, valuing those people above any other people, was clinging to a worldly luxury. He meant you have to put away those protections and comforts and follow Him. It's not unlike what the Buddha said. As I've pointed out to Sylvia. Stop celebrating your own personal tribe and planning weenie roasts for your own special circle of favorite people and concentrate on what Jesus actually said, and maybe you'll actually find Him.

Monica Faithful The day of the party dawned. The weather couldn't have been better if I'd ordered it from Tiffany. Most everything was taken care of except doing the flowers. The garden was blooming its head off. I'd had my

tea and toast and been down to cut what I needed for cen-
terpieces and bouquets for the Porta Potti, which we hoped
people would use, because otherwise the well would go dry
from flushing.

I was out on the porch with my bucket of dahlias and
larkspur and cosmos and lilies, thinking about Mother and
how many thousands of times she had stood here, with
these very shears and vases and the ancestors of these very
flowers, all chosen and nurtured by her, and how much she
had loved all that, when Regis appeared. He'd come to tell
me that Toto had barfed on the stairs.

I said I was actually quite busy and where were his parents? Meditating, said Regis. In their room, on their zafus.

I said, "Well, how about if you clean it up?" I told him I
bet he could do that. He looked extremely doubtful. I told
him to go to Shirley and get a bowl of water, and a roll of
paper towels, and after I was finished with my flowers, we
would spray rug shampoo on the place and later I'd let him
use the new vacuum cleaner. Boys like machines, don't
they? I didn't see why he shouldn't learn to clean up after
his own dog.

About ten minutes later I went in to see how he was
making out. He was sitting on the stairs, and behind him
there were two pools of barf, one from the puppy and one
from Regis. Guess who got to clean *that* up.

Norman Faithful And it was hot in Union and jammed
with tourists on their way to Mount Desert, or such places.
America in Bermuda shorts is not a pretty sight. But I had
an interesting thought on the way home. Although Jesus
teaches that we must put away family (yes, yes, and pride,

and greed and envy and all those emotions that spring from our attachments to worldly things), but I mean, He actually says you must stop loving your mother and father, in order to love Him, that He nevertheless describes the structure of God, the nature of God, in family terms? God is a father and a son and a cloud of family love? The Buddha doesn't do that. The Buddha says that if you put away worldly distractions, like where are you going to sleep tonight and where your next meal is coming from, and whether or not your brother-in-law's dog is going to eat your shoes, and concentrate, that you will find God within yourself. That God dwells within you *as* yourself... no, that may be Hindu. Anyway.

Is that how Jesus gets captured by the Family Values guys? Because he describes God as a father? Kind of a risky strategy, really. How you're going to relate to that God depends an awful lot on what kind of father you had personally. Certainly the Greeks and Romans saw the gods in family groups, but not as role models. I mean, Zeus was always down at the mall boffing the checkout girls.

Monica Faithful I really needed to zip to town to get some carpet shampoo, but of course Norman had our car. I had to borrow Shirley's. Which I hate to do because what if I bang it up? And also because at some point a pot of chowder she was taking to a potluck spilled in it, and you never really get a smell like that out of the upholstery. Thank God, Cinder and Marta were there when I got back. They took over the flowers while I ironed tablecloths and napkins. Shirley is a saint among women but she does not iron.

Josslyn Moss I decided the way I could help most was to get everyone out of Monica's way, so we took the children and Toto to the bathing beach for a picnic lunch and then to climb Butter Hill. And then for ice cream, double scoop for Regis, since Aunt Monica made him throw up. Nothing like feeling in the way in your own house.

Marta Rowland We knew we were in the clear to go help Nika, because Bobby had taken Ellie sailing for the day. Cinder and I had pretty much exhausted the possibilities for amusement down the Quarry Road. It was nice to be able to go to town. We did the flowers and then we all did the seating together. Monica was planning to put Rufus Maitland at the head table with El and Bobby. Cinder and I looked at each other and then we both said, Oh, no no no no no no no no.

Monica Faithful At four in the afternoon, the caterer came to tell me that the stove wouldn't light. I had been just about to go up for my bath. I assumed they didn't know they had to use the clicker to light the burners. Or at worst that the oven pilot was out. But oh no. Oh, it couldn't be anything that simple. I called Plumbing and Heating and got no answer so I called Al Pease at home. I must have sounded like an hysteric.

Al Pease The last time I got an emergency call to that house, there was two dead people in the upstairs bathroom, so I listened carefully. Seems she was giving a wingding and the world was going to end if the stove didn't work this minute. When I got her calmed down, I said, "Monica, is there a smell of gas in the kitchen?" She said there was, and it was strong. You'd think people would call you before they blew themselves up, wouldn't you? It must have been smelling for days. I said, "Sounds to me like you're out of propane." Well, she went straight up and turned left.

Monica Faithful Al drove the propane truck right out himself and filled the tank up. I asked him how could that have happened, didn't we get regular deliveries? I'd never known that to happen, ever. He said he couldn't tell, maybe the bills weren't paid, maybe somebody took us off the schedule by mistake. Cressida would know, but she was down in Boston visiting their daughter. Who were they sending the bills to? Al didn't know.

Al Pease You know, propane doesn't have a smell. You add that smell to it so people will know it if there's a leak. When you get to the bottom of the tank the smell is pretty much what's left so it gets stronger. Doesn't anyone in this family know when to call the plumber?

Monica Faithful Edith and Nora had gone out sailing with Bobby and El, to help Bobby keep her out of our way. They got back to Leeway at about six, said that El was having a shower. She thought Bobby was taking her to dinner down on Little Deer. People started arriving at six-fifteen—they all had to park down at the Gantrys' or wherever they could, so the driveway wouldn't be full of cars. I even made them hide the catering truck. Upstairs Adam and Alison and Edie were rushing in and out of bedrooms, borrowing toothpaste and hair dryers from each other. So much fun. The puppy was entirely overexcited by all the people in the house and had to be locked in the laundry room. Norman said he couldn't handle it and went down to the gazebo with a beer and a book. We gave him Marta for a dinner partner.

Bobby Applegate My biggest problem was going to be keeping El from going in through the kitchen, the way we always did. If she saw the catering stuff the jig would be up, because Nika would never ever give a big party without inviting her sister. What I finally did was, I stopped the car at the front porch and went, "Ohmigod, did you see that?" And jumped out and ran to the lawn. Of course El followed me, saying, "What? What?" I told her I'd seen a bobcat. There have been sightings this summer, but not on the Point. So then there we were at the front stairs and I took her elbow and took her up to the porch.

Monica Faithful Edie was on the watch from the upstairs bedroom. She ran down to tell us when the car turned into the driveway. So here we were all crammed together in the living room, trying not to sneeze or giggle or rattle our drinks. I was nearly dead from excitement. I'd never done this before, pulled off a surprise. It seemed to take forever for their footsteps to come up to the porch. Then finally the door swung open and there they were, framed in the doorway with the light behind them, and everyone yelled, "Surprise!"

Eleanor Applegate I was absolutely appalled.

Monica Faithful And she looked at us and then burst into tears. Adam went and gave her a kiss and said, "Happy birthday, Mom." He was so pleased. And she looked at him as if she couldn't understand who he was or what he was doing there. Everyone was asking, "Were you really surprised?" and Eleanor just spluttered. Finally, she said, "Totally."

Marta Rowland Dinner was pretty late, owing to the propane fiasco, so everyone was well oiled by the time we sat down, but only Homer Gantry was completely plastered. The children and Bobby all made charming speeches, and Eleanor rose to the occasion. Uncle Homer made a toast about lovely Eleanor and her lovely parents that made no sense at all, but his children made him sit down. How on earth has he lived to be that old, still drinking like that? I got along all right with Norman and learned a great deal about where Thomas à Becket's bones aren't. I guess all preachers are actors. He enjoyed booming, "Will no one rid me of this troublesome priest?"

Cinder Smart I had Rufus Maitland for a dinner partner, so I had a wonderful time. Who wouldn't? He doesn't know I know about him and Eleanor.

Marta Rowland El would have run off with him. It was Rufus who wouldn't let her, even though he adored her. In fact, I guess that's a measure of how *much* he adored her. He knew something about himself that she didn't.

Cinder Smart How did Bobby forgive her? I have no idea. I've known women who have done it, but never a man.

Marta Rowland I'd say it's partly because they never told anyone else. Bobby doesn't even know we know. But when Eleanor thought she was going to leave the children she had to talk to someone. I said if she talked to me, she had to tell Cinder too. I could promise not to tell my husband, but I had to be allowed to tell someone.

El and Bobby's was one of those marriages that everyone counts on and looks to. The one that proves marriage can work.

Cinder Smart I was stunned at the time. Looking back, I think I understand it. When we were at school, she and Rufus were like Hansel and Gretel or something, they were practically children when they fell for each other. There's nothing quite so pure as that feeling but in a way it's unbearable. She was plunged into despair if he didn't write. The whole dorm was excited when he came to call on her, hanging out the windows to watch them going off on their walk, poking each other and laughing as if they were bear cubs. He was such a romantic figure, even then, the handsome bad boy. Of course it couldn't stand up to real life. Of course they broke up about six times. Then she fell for Bobby, and that was real.

Marta Rowland I thought the problem was she was so innocent when she married Bobby. He was her first ... you know. So when it was all so easy and smooth she began to mistrust it. The view of marriage she'd grown up with was anything but. I mean her parents were polite, they always behaved, but even a child could see how much work it must have been for them, they were so different, so that's what she thought marriage was really like. Difficult. And then every summer, there was Rufus, the one who got away. What had she lost, what had she missed? And he was lonely. He's chosen a lonely life.

Cinder Smart It was terrible when he gave her up. You might think the love of two good men would be a great thing, but I never will again. It's horrible to be divided like that. I feared for her sanity, I really did.

Marta Rowland And Monica doesn't know. That stuns me. She was in Oregon or Colorado while this was going on, but not all the time, and there was a *lot* of pain. A lot of tears. How on earth did El keep that in the box when her sister was around? Of course she had to ... I mean, if she was staying with Bobby, the family couldn't know. But I wonder why Monica thinks Eleanor and Bobby started having babies again, after all those years.

Cinder Smart That was Bobby's deal. New babies, a new start. That and silence. And obviously, they've stuck to it.

Norman Faithful I'd say the party was a great success, if you like that sort of bunfight, and don't count the fact that the well went dry.

Josslyn Moss Nobody used the Porta Potti. Every single person there had been in and out of Leeway all their lives and thought, Well, this PLEASE KEEP OUT sign in the bathroom can't mean *me* . . .

Monica Faithful We had no idea about the well, until the caterer's girl came to tell me there was no water so they couldn't wash the dishes. I went out to the kitchen and sure enough . . . I told them to stack things and we'd deal with it in the morning. They cleared up and went home. In the living room, the band was roaring and everyone was dancing. The children were mostly dancing out on the porch until Rufus Maitland came in and said to me, "You know, that porch is a hundred years old—I think you may have a critical load out there." I said, "Oh dear," so he went out and told the children either to come in or dance on the lawn, and of course they didn't mind that at all.

Rufus Maitland I'd been at a party down the Neck where the porch steps tore right off the deck, just as three old ladies were coming down the stairs with plates in their hands. Aunt Gladdy must have fallen five feet. Three of them ass over teakettle, all in a heap and covered in crab salad. No bones were broken and nobody sued, but that was a miracle.

A little while later I was dancing with Nika and she said, "And of course now the well's gone dry too." We'd all had a lot to drink, so she was cheerful about it. I said, "So you've turned the pump off?" She boogied along for a while and then she said, "What pump?"

Jimmy Moss Rufus Maitland and I ended up in the pitch-black crawl space underneath the house with flashlights, creeping around on damp ledge and spiders and worse, trying to find the circuit box. It's in the far corner, under the kitchen. Someone had labeled the switches in the dim past; it's Pop's writing, I think, but some labels were missing. I tried one, and from the sudden silence upstairs, followed by pandemonium, we knew we'd hit the power to the living room. I flipped it and the music started again. Rufus said, "That was kind of fun." Finally we found the switch for the well pump and turned it off, but Rufus said he'd be pretty surprised if we hadn't burned it out, and of course, come the dawn, we had.

Bobby Applegate In the car on the way home, Eleanor said to me, "Can you make me a promise?" I said, "What?" She said, "That you won't ever let anyone do that to me again, ever?" I said, "Yes, I can do that."

Eleanor Applegate When I was about nine, Mother gave me a surprise party for my birthday. She invited all her friends' children and some houseguests' children nobody knew. There were too many people, too many ages, she planned games we were too old for and none of them was fun, the houseguests' children cried, and the birthday cake was cheesecake and everybody hated it. Amelia's job was to take me off to the library or something and then bring me home at the right moment. It took me weeks to forgive her. Oh, and, Mother didn't want the houseguests' children to be embarrassed they didn't have presents for me, so no one was allowed to bring presents. I was miserable. What I wanted to do on my birthday was choose three friends and go to Union to see a movie. Or have a slumber party. Not games. Not strangers. Not creamed chicken and peas. She did it to me two years in a row. When you grow up with a parent who can blow up without warning, you don't like enormous changes at the last moment.

It always seemed to me that the people who yell "Surprise!" the loudest are the ones who like you least.

Bobby Applegate I don't blame Monica. I know she was trying to do a good thing. Some people love surprises. I didn't know for sure Eleanor wouldn't like it. If I didn't, Nika didn't. And El was very happy afterward, to have all her children and Cinder and Marta with her.

Eleanor Applegate Where was Monica for those birthdays? In camp? She has to have been there. Did I not tell her how much I hated it? How could she not remember? Was she just so glad that Mother was doing something horrible to someone besides her that it didn't register?

Monica Faithful It was the party of the summer. Some years there just is one, and for sure this year it was Eleanor's surprise party. When a party like that really comes off, and even the helpers are beaming and the whole house roars with happiness, it's all worth it.

Shirley Eaton I came in the next morning and it looked as if every plate and cup in the house had been used and left for me to wash. There were stacks all over the kitchen and pantry. I said to Mr. Faithful, "What am I supposed to do about this, with no water?" He said, "I haven't the faintest idea," and went off down the lawn. Never much help, that one.

Jimmy Moss I loved the party and so did the children. Though we all got up late and the kids did seem to have hangovers, they'd had so much sugar and excitement, which Josslyn wasn't best pleased about. I called Al Pease and told him about the pump being burned out and asked him if he knows where the pump *is*. He said it's down in the well, buried out on the lawn, and he'd send his son Jeff out to dig it out.

Jeff Pease I had the well uncovered by the time Jimmy Moss wandered out. It was a hot day and that was not pleasant work. The wellhead was old and weighed about a ton, and I'd given it a couple of heaves without moving it. Jimmy put down his coffee and got down in the hole with me and we both heaved. By the time we got it off and started pulling the pump up a hundred and forty-seven feet Jimmy's wife come out in her bathrobe and she says, "Jimmy, you be careful you don't put your back out."

What about *my* back? I'm older than he is.

Josslyn Moss They got the thing out, finally, and the plumber drove away with *it*, and Jimmy went upstairs and took four Advil. We were supposed to play tennis that afternoon. There went that idea.

Al Pease I drove to Bangor for a new pump that would fit that system, while Patty took Jeff to the hospital for a cortisone shot. He had to lie down in the back of the truck to get there, but the shot fixed him up, at least so he could walk.

Shirley Eaton The well finally filled back up and I had water by the next day. I'd carried most of the dishes home with me to wash. Monica filled jugs at the town pump for their drinking water and they ate lunch and dinner out. We all used the Porta Potti that day, except the children kept forgetting, so the upstairs flush got stopped and we had to call Al Pease again. Being a plumber's a wonderful life, don't you think?

Josslyn Moss I didn't know what the bills were going to look like, but I knew I wasn't going to pay them. It wasn't my party, and it certainly wasn't me who didn't have the sense to turn the pump off. Why didn't anyone tell *me* the well was dry? What is it, I don't live here too?

Cressida Pease I sent the bills to Norman Faithful. The Applegates don't use Leeway and I don't have Jimmy Moss's address, what else was I supposed to do? And nobody paid them, so I took them off the delivery schedule. Al's some irked with me. I know, I should have called someone. But I couldn't abide Sydney Moss and I didn't relish being treated like that by another generation.

Eleanor Applegate When they had the water back on, Bobby and I went down to Leeway for lunch on the porch with Nika and Norman. Shirley brought everything out on trays, and we sat side by side looking down to the bay, the way Mother and Papa used to do. I don't know if the others were thinking of them, but they were very much with me. How much they both loved this view. The flag was on the breeze, the gardens were gorgeous. Jimmy's children were playing down in the field the way we used to. If Papa were here, he'd be getting ready to go out on the *Stone* to watch the sailing races in the afternoon. I said, "Since so many of us are in town, shouldn't we make plans to take the ashes out and let them go?"

Monica Faithful I'd been thinking the same thing. Only Sylvie and Sam were missing, and Edie could stay another day. Norman could do the prayers. We'd take the ashes out to the middle of the bay, where Papa used to take us to troll for mackerel when we were little. And Mother used to yell at us how to trim our sails when we were racing Turn-abouts.

Jimmy Moss "Trim! Trim! Trim, Monica!" you could hear Mom shouting all over the fleet. It still makes us laugh.

Monica Faithful El and I played golf in the afternoon, and made a little list of who should come with us. Aunt Gladdy and Uncle Neville, of course. The Henneberrys. The Gantrys wouldn't come, but we'd ask them.

Eleanor Applegate I thought we should ask Papa's poker group, Mutt Dodge, Al Pease, and so on. It would make the group too big for the *Stone,* but the Maitlands' boatman would probably come along in *Woodwind.* That boat could take a few dozen.

Monica Faithful Most of the people we wanted to include were at the club that afternoon, as they were most afternoons, so we didn't have to make many phone calls. The oldies were up on the porch playing bridge or watching the croquet. The others were on the golf course or playing tennis. Aunt Elise said Of course about *Woodwind*, so we put the word out that we'd leave the dock at two the next afternoon, and anyone who wanted to come was welcome.

Eleanor Applegate After dinner that night at Leeway, I was going through Papa's poetry books looking for something to read. His favorite poem in English was "The Cremation of Sam McGee," which was all too appropriate, but we decided to save it for the gathering afterward. Monica was trying to write something for the service. Nora was sorting through her boxes looking for just the right pictures of Mother and Papa to take along, when Norman took a phone call.

Monica Faithful He came back in and announced he had to go home. He'd booked the early flight out of Bangor. I was upset, I really was. Apparently there was going to be an intervention on one of his parishioners, Rebecca Vogelsang. I didn't even know she drank. But Norman said her husband and children all agreed, and they all thought he had to be there. I said I didn't see why—Lindsay Tautsch could handle it. He said it wasn't like that. It had to be all the people the person really cares about, saying the same thing at once.

I pointed out that tomorrow was important to *this* family too. He was going to read the prayers. These were my parents. He said he was very, very sorry, but there was a life to be saved, and he had to go.

Eleanor Applegate You know what? I thought, Good. Go away. Hugh Chamblee really loved our father; I'd rather have him do it anyway. Monica was terribly disappointed, though.

Elise Maitland Henneberry It was a body blow to me, losing Sydney and Laurus. Of course Sydney hadn't been herself for some time, so I suppose you could say it was a release for her, but I never felt she hated what had happened to her mind, as so many people do. At the end she had a sweetness she'd never really shown before. She trusted Laurus to love her and make good plans for them both. And she enjoyed the sun, and her food, and seeing familiar faces. She had an appetite for life still. And Laurus! How I loved that man. Sydney made mistakes in her life, but she got the most important thing right when she married him. They are missed. So of course I was glad the children asked for *Woodwind.*

We had quite a time getting Homer Gantry aboard; it took Kermit and Al Pease pulling together and Rufus pushing from behind to do it. Charlesie had the *Rolling Stone* all dressed, with pennants up the forestay to the top of the mast, and down the back. And he was flying Laurus's blue flag on the jackstaff, from the years he was commodore. Syl Conary had run the blue flag up the club flagpole too, as Laurus left the dock for the last time.

Charlesie led the way under power out of the inner

harbor, and we followed. The three Moss children sat together in the cockpit of the *Rolling Stone,* and most of the grandchildren were sitting along the deck up in the bow, with their legs dangling over the gunwales. Eleanor's oldest two, Adam and Annie, came with me, and Adam's girl Alison Boyd. I used to know her mother, Susanna Boyd, in New York. A lovely person.

Chris sat beside me and held my hand. Someday not so long from now it will be our children, and we'll be the ones in the urns. I hope all these beautiful young people come along on a day just like this, to see us off.

Eleanor Applegate We got out into the middle of the bay and *Woodwind* came alongside so we could gam together. Jimmy asked Hugh Chamblee to begin. Hugh put on his patchwork stole, and stood in the stern of the *Woodwind.* The boats rocked a little. Uncle Neville wore his golf hat and Aunt Gladdy and Aunt Elise both had dresses and big straw hats on. Monica and I were wearing sunglasses and so was Al Pease, a sight I hadn't seen before. Monica had one urn, and I had the other one. There were stickers on the bottom telling which was which, but we hadn't looked. It didn't seem right to turn them over and read the labels, as if they were pickled beets.

Hugh said a prayer, and then read the committal from Mother's prayer book. Ashes to ashes, dust to dust, in the midst of life we are in death. Then we opened the urns—Charlesie had to help us, they'd stuck the lids on tight—and leaning over the leeward rail, we began to pour. We hadn't talked about how we would do this; we just did it together that way, and the breeze took the ashes and mixed them together as they fell. When we were done we looked at the labels. I had had Papa, and Nika had Mother. We rinsed the urns out with seawater, so it would be completely over.

Then Monica tried to read "Nothing Gold Can Stay," the poem she had read when we did this for Aunt Nina, and Mother and Papa were with us, but she couldn't. She was a mess. Jimmy took the book from her and read it. Then we started the engines again, and went home.

· V ·

THE PRODIGAL SON

Jimmy Moss

Papa.

In the Amazon, I was born from a tree, whose roots I'd seen, whose head reached all the way to the jungle canopy, my blood was sap. Hearing about other people's sacred visions is like listening to people talk about a movie you haven't seen. They may want to make you see what they saw, but they just can't.

So. Later, in San Francisco.

I'd moved out of the Haight, and had a little apartment down in the Mission. It was a barrio, and I liked that. I'd started reading again, which I hadn't done much of since seventh grade or some such. Reading for me used to be like sweating and rolling a huge rock up a hill, while all around me my little friends were whisking past me up to the top in a trice, swinging their berry buckets and whistling Dixie. I just stopped doing it, right in the middle of *David* fucking *Copperfield*. But alone in a room, after where I'd been, it didn't matter if I was slower than anybody else, nobody else was there. It was only me and the words. Barkis was willing.

It became my new addiction. The main library at Civic Center was my university, and I thought I'd die happy if I could sit there learning about astronomy and Darwin and the lives of the saints for the rest of my life. But I was running out of money. And at that point, after years, one day my father knocked on my door. My earthly father, not the tree fellow.

I don't know how he found me. Nika, probably, though she says not. He came in. He walked around looking at things. Stacks of books. Half-drunk mugs of tea abandoned here and there. A mattress on the floor, bed unmade. I offered him some herb tea, and he accepted.

When I came out of the kitchen with the mugs, he was sitting in the only chair, beside my stump, studying my book stack. My book table was a tree stump. It came with the apartment. I sat down on my zafu. I didn't have visitors as a rule, so one chair had been enough up to then.

In the years since I'd been home, I'd pictured meeting them again, my parents who were dead to me, and always pictured them asking questions and then not understanding the answers. In my head I used to work on my answers to the questions they'd ask, about where I'd gone, and what I thought I was doing with my life, and I'd end up angry that I couldn't get it quite right, and besides, that they were putting me in the position of having to try. But he didn't ask me anything. He just looked at things, like a stranger with good manners. Finally I asked him what he was doing in San Francisco, and he said he was giving a recital that night at Herbst Auditorium. I waited for him to ask me to come, but he didn't. I asked him how everyone was at home. He said everyone was well. My nephew Adam was talking. I'd sort of forgotten that Adam existed.

It was weirdly peaceful to have him there. He was comfortable with silence, and he was comfortable with me. It was very surprising. He looked at my stuff, my tiny world, without needing to comment. He hadn't come to judge, he'd just come to see, and let it be. I had no idea he had that quality. I'd never noticed.

After he left, I went back to sit in the chair, to see my room through his eyes. I saw that he'd moved some of the books. One I had from the library was a Bible, King James Version. I'd been reading about David and Jonathan. I picked it up and it opened to the Twenty-third Psalm. Not very surprising; I read it a lot. Why does it switch from He to Thou, the way it does? He restoreth me, he leadeth me, but in the valley of the shadow of death *thou* art with me. Who is David talking to? Is it David, really? His voice?

But that afternoon, I saw something I'd read a hundred times and never understood. "Thou preparest a table before me in the presence of mine enemies: thou anointest my head with oil; my cup runneth over."

Why in the presence of my enemies? It seemed like a divisive thing for the Lord to do, to prepare a table for me while they eat their hearts out. God as schoolyard bully. And then I saw what it meant. The point is that he prepares the table for *me*. He has no choice but to do it in the presence of my enemies, because I insist upon carrying them around with me.

I went to Herbst. My father seemed like an alternate version of himself, wearing white tie and tails. He walked onto the stage to a roar of applause, and I had no more relationship to him than anyone else in the hall. He seemed shiny, his smile, his high forehead, his bright white shirt. I didn't look at the program, I wanted to find out what would happen as he came to it.

He started with the Chopin B-flat Minor Sonata, the one with the funeral march—very big, stormy work. Then, the polar opposite, the Webern Variations—short, sparse, atonal—almost otherworldly after the Chopin. The third piece was the Mozart B Minor Adagio, another very short piece which he started almost without pause and without applause after the Webern. The two textures were so alike, I wasn't quite sure what it was, whether he was still in the Variations—it was radical, how modern the Mozart sounded. The program was like a funnel, starting with the huge deluge of the Chopin and distilling down from Webern to a simple B minor triad in the low bass in the Mozart.

I don't remember the intermission.

The second half was the Schubert D Major Sonata, op. 53, only dimly familiar to me at that time. It's a long four-movement piece, very emotional and melodic. To go from the depth of the Chopin, through the thin tunnel of the Webern and Mozart, and into the sunshine of Schubert opened me up as if it were a can opener. I went home and cried for a day and a half.

Monica Faithful I expected Norman to come back up to Maine when they got Beccy Vogelsang off to the hat factory, but he didn't. He said he had to go down to check on his mother. Then there were other excuses. I figured the hell with him. Adam and Alison announced their engagement the night after we scattered Mother and Papa. Adam said it really got to him, watching those ashes blow together. At sunset, he took Alison down to our gazebo and proposed. Then they went out to the Salt Pond to tell Eleanor and Bobby, and El invited us all to dinner the next night, with Amelia and Barbara and Aunt Gladdy and Uncle Neville. There was champagne, there were tears. The first of the grandkids to marry. Bobby is going to give them his mother's engagement ring when they get home, which made Eleanor cry. Everyone loved Bobby's mother.

The one little burr I've got in my sock about this, which I'll tell you, but no one else, is that some time in the week of the party for Eleanor, a little carved ivory elephant that was on the mantelpiece at Leeway disappeared. I know there were a lot of people in and out, but I'd seen Alison pick it up and study it more than once. I'm just so sorry I know that thing about her mother.

The elephant was something Sydney bought in India, when she and her mother went around the world after our grandfather died. It had tiny little black bead ebony eyes. Nora just lately came across an entry in Mother's trip diary from the day she bought it. I think they were in Jaipur. It's not valuable, but it reminded me of her and it's always been there on the mantelpiece. You know.

Adam Applegate When I got back to D.C. I told everyone at work I was engaged; I couldn't resist. One of the senior partners, Leonard Rashbaum, asked me where the wedding would be, and I said, "Dundee, Maine, next July," and he said, "Dundee, Maine. I used to know someone who went to Dundee, Maine. Her name was Monica Moss." I went, "Monica Moss is my aunt! The wedding will be at her house!" And he said, "Really?" And I said I hoped so, and he said, "I'd like to be invited." Can you believe that? It feels like magic. Dundee magic. I don't know if he was serious, but we're going to invite him anyway.

Sylvia Faithful Things had been really busy at the restaurant. August is usually dead, but we were full and the manager broke his ankle so all the rest of us were filling in. Plus, I'd been busy breaking up with my boyfriend. I finally got a week off and went up to Leeway. I missed the big surprise party for Eleanor, and Adam getting engaged. I was in time for the Brouhaha of the Pillows, however.

Bobby Applegate I drove up to the dump with the whole car full of trash and recycling. I go around to do the recycling first. Have you been up to the dump? Pardon me, transfer station? I sort of love it. The smell isn't for everyone, but it's a part of life you don't see if you live in the city. One area is for construction debris. There's a lot of that of course. Town planning runs against the Yankee grain, so we're in the grip of our own little blight of suburban sprawl. There's another for satellite dishes, you know those huge black ones that sit on your lawn, the size of a barn door? Now that everyone has little pizza dishes attached to their roofs, the old ones have formed an obsolescence club up there. Then there's the shed where you dump your paper, your glass, and your tins and plastic. I enjoy chatting with the transfer guys. Boy, do they see a lot. Counting the bottles.

When I finished there, I drove up to the garbage pits, which are chutes lined with crushers, and man, they do *not* smell good. The seagulls love it. I see the ancient truck from Leeway is there. Usually it's Marlon who does the dump runs for Leeway, and just as well because the transmission on that truck is about gone and you have to have a surgeon's touch to find third gear. But it's not Marlon, it's Josslyn, and what she is throwing into the garbage pit is all Sydney's down pillows. I swear, I almost jumped in after them. Do you know what a good down pillow costs? I know Jimmy loves her but sometimes I wonder if she has the sense God gave a goose.

Josslyn Moss Boedie's had a stuffed-up nose since we got here, and her eyes itch. I've never had down pillows. Old feathers? It sounds filthy. Plus they've been in an unheated house all winter for years. Mold, hello? I think foam is healthier, and I asked Shirley Eaton if down was safe and she said she uses foam.

Monica Faithful Bobby told Eleanor and she came roaring down to Leeway on the double and told me. We ran upstairs, and sure enough, every down pillow in the house was gone. There must have been two dozen of them! Mother always kept foam pillows in the linen closet for guests who were allergic.

Eleanor Applegate When Josslyn came in the door, we happened to be standing there in the living room, and I'm afraid we let her have it.

Monica Faithful Which we shouldn't have done, I admit that, it was a timing thing. But holy moly and the horse she rode in on, why didn't she ask first? We *are* sharing this house, aren't we?

Eleanor Applegate Why didn't she give Boedie a foam pillow and leave the rest alone?!

Josslyn Moss That's it. I'm done. I can't share a house with those bitches. Everything I do is wrong, no one ever asks me about anything, I wasn't raised in a barn, you know. I come from somewhere too. This isn't working. End of experiment.

Jimmy Moss Josslyn didn't know. She thought she was helping. I put the whole family in the car and we went to Union to the water slides. While the kids were playing, Joss and I talked through it. Then we stopped at Wal-Mart on the way home and bought two dozen of the best foam pillows they had, and I promised my sisters I'd have a dozen down ones sent from some catalogue in the morning.

It made me sad, though. I think it's good for the family, all the cousins, sharing the house, and Nika and I enjoy the hubbub. But Josslyn doesn't. She just can't, and she shouldn't have to.

Sylvia Faithful I was sorting through picture albums with Nora—we were doing Candace's family—when I thought to ask, "Where are the urns? Sydney and Laurus's ashes?" I'd noticed they weren't on the mantel. Nora said, "We scattered them on the bay last week." And I said, "What?"

You What?

Monica Faithful She was devastated. I had no idea she'd be so upset... I mean I see now that I *should* have known. At the time, I think I just thought we're only missing two of the grandchildren. We better do this while we can. I didn't stop to think that the two we were missing were the ones who most feel that they don't really belong. I could shoot myself.

Josslyn Moss I knew it was a mistake. Too bad no one asks me anything.

Eleanor Applegate I went down to Leeway to help Nika explain to Sylvie how it was—there was so much going on, we did what seemed best at the time. It was so too bad that neither Sylvie or Sam could come for the famous surprise party, then they'd have been here too.

Sylvia Faithful Earth to Eleanor. I was working. You know, *working*? I don't know how all the rest of them man-age to take off for weeks in the summer, but I have a job. So does Sam. Can you say "trust fund"?

Monica Faithful She left that night. She left me a thank-you note, on Leeway Cottage letter paper. It said, "Thanks a lot." Oh God.

Nora Applegate I told Sylvie about the ashes, and she started to cry. My big cousin, the one who is always cool. I guess you're never too old to have your family hurt your feelings. She said, "You know, Grandma Sydney loved Sam and me as much as the rest of you. She always always treated us the same." And I said, "Sylvie, she couldn't stand any of us! She didn't like children!" And she got up and left the room, crying. I guess that wasn't so helpful.

She must be having a really hard summer.

Sylvia Faithful I took the bus home. It's longer, but much cheaper and people are less likely to interfere with you if you're crying or something. By the time I got to Connecticut I realized that the one I was really pissed at was my father. He was there when they decided that everyone who counted was in town. He must have known how this would feel to me. Why the hell didn't he say something?

Norman Faithful Mary McCarthy once wrote, "I am driven to the conclusion that religion is only good for good people. For others, it is too great a temptation to the deadly sins of pride and anger, chiefly, but one might also add sloth." Isn't that wonderful?

My curate is either not a simpatico person or not well suited to this parish. And of course once you've got an Iago in a church, it is all too easy for that little sliver of fallen angel to find ready disciples to do the devil's work. It simply amazes me that people think that Satan is a mythological concept. How do they explain what they see all around them? Oh, Satan is having himself a most joyous little century.

There's not much one can do in August, however. The bishop is on Martha's Vineyard and most of the vestry is gone as well. I had to stay where I was and try to keep the lid on the pot and be a healing presence. So I sat in my office and read up on the Arian Heresy. I think there's a new book in it. We don't actually have any writings from the Arians themselves, as you probably know, since all their texts were destroyed. We have to piece together what they thought from those who denounced them. History is written by the victors.

To put it simply, the Arians believed that Jesus has not always existed, but was created by God. This horrified the

Trinitarians, the One God in Three Persons boys, because it smacked of polytheism. And makes Jesus somehow subordinate to God. But it's so interesting. Was Jesus created? Was there a time before He existed, as there was with the rest of us? If so, and He was both divine and fully human, did He know from inception that He was God, or did his knowledge of his divinity accrue, as it certainly appears from close reading of the Gospels? His moments of feeling deeply separate from God seem to me to be exactly what makes Him so approachable to the rest of us.

And then the real question is how to define and describe the Holy Spirit. God plus Jesus alive in us all in present time, but how to make that feel real? How to see the living God, the risen Christ, looking out of the eyes of every person we meet? You could have a blessed and holy life riding the New York subways all day long, trying to live by that one thought. A monastic plan the Buddha would approve. And if you succeeded, you'd be a saint. They'd have a room all ready for you and painted your favorite color when you got to Heaven. You can't do something like that, really do it, without being profoundly changed, and that of course changes the world you move in. In the way Jesus meant us to. Maybe that's the book—*A Priest's Year in the Subway*. That sounds better than *Arian Heresy*, doesn't it?

Where was I?

Anyway, I was working when Sam called me to tell me that his mother was in the hospital. Apparently she tried to kill herself. And I thought, really, How long, oh Lord? How long is this test going to take? It's been one thing after another for months now. Just pile it on me, Lord, you want to see how much it takes to get me on my knees? Rachel, Rachel, Rachel.

Monica Faithful Sam called Leeway, looking for his sister. I had to tell him she'd gone back to New York suddenly, and I told him why and apologized to him too about the ashes, but he barely registered it. He said his aunt Lynn had called to say their mother is in the ICU. I think Aunt Lynn is the one who never married and makes hats. Sam was on a cell phone and it was hard to hear. He wasn't even in Los Angeles, he was up in the Sierra on location. He couldn't leave for a day, and when he could it was going to take him forever to get back to civilization and onto a plane to Boston. I told him to do whatever he had to do, and I'd find Sylvie. She wasn't answering her cell, which I understood when I found it on the floor of my car the next morning. She must have lost it when Marlon drove her over to Union to catch the bus. I reached her at work in the evening.

Sam had told me where Rachel was and I'd called for an update on her condition. She was still alive, but hadn't regained consciousness. She must have made a very serious attempt. Naturally, Sylvie was stunned. I could hear the hubbub of the restaurant behind her but at first she didn't say a word. I said that I assumed she'd want to go to Boston right away, and I said, "Do you want your father to go with you?" and she said, "That asshole?"

I let it pass. But she shouldn't have to do this alone. I said, "Shall I come?" and she said yes, which almost made me cry. I said, "Tonight?" And she was undone, she said no, she had to work her shift, then yes, then no again. I told her I'd be at the hospital by noon, and would wait for her in the waiting room. Of course I couldn't go near Rachel myself, that would be too strange.

Sylvia Faithful It was a terrible night at work. I kept forgetting things, I was really out of it. She is my mother. She is my *mother*. I wished she could learn to take care of herself so I didn't have to worry about her all the damn time, but she is my mother. I thought how hard I'd been on her, and what if she really was doing the best she could?

I got home about one and tried to sleep, but I couldn't. So I got back up and booked a ticket on the first Acela to Boston. I was able to sleep a little on the train, because it was in motion and because there was nothing else I could do, except be on my way. I barely had enough money for the taxi to the hospital, I'd forgotten to stop at a cash machine. My brain wasn't working right. All I could think was, she couldn't be dead. She had to be alive when I got there.

Nika was in the waiting room of the ICU. She hugged me. She said Mommy was responding a little. She had squeezed the doctor's fingers when he told her to.

I went down to Mommy's room, and they made me put on a gown and rubber gloves. Aunt Lynn was there, and my granma, who was crying. Aunt Lynn got up and kissed me, and whispered, "Finally." The kiss that meant, What took you so long and where is your brother? Granma held Mommy's hand and sniffled. Granma is so little that perched on that plastic chair, her feet didn't touch the floor. Mommy had a tube in her nose and another stuck with a needle into the back of her hand and she looked waxy. Her hair was dirty and her fingernails were all ragged. That scared me almost the most. Mommy's hands were always beautiful. Always.

Aunt Lynn gave me her chair and left the room. I took Mommy's hand and sat there. I started talking to her. I said, "Mommy, it's Sylvie. I'm here. Sam's on the way. You're doing great. It's going to be fine." Then I'd say it over again. I said, "Mommy, squeeze my hand," and I think she tried to. I said, "Mommy, it's Sylvie. Say hello to me. Mommy, say 'Sylvie,'" and I saw something, her eyelids moved, and she turned her head toward me a little. Then she slipped back and was deep under again.

Aunt Lynn came back in and I said, "Lynn, she recognized my voice! She turned toward me!" And Lynn made a gesture that I should step out into the hall with her. She shut the door behind us and then she said, "Sylvie, who the hell is that woman in the waiting room?"

Monica Faithful Of course I knew it was odd for me to be there. But Sylvie would get no comfort from her aunt or her grandmother. It wasn't a happy family. Rachel and the sisters fought a great deal and the mother didn't help. They hated me for taking Norman away from Rachel, which I don't think I did, but when they weren't doing that, they were blaming Rachel for losing him. And they all were bitter about Sam and Sylvie's summers at Leeway. There was plenty of reason on their side and plenty of blame for all, but what there wasn't was comfort for Sam or Sylvie.

I remember Sylvie saying that she had learned from us to put salt on her cantaloupe. I don't know where that comes from, Mother did it, we always did it. It makes it taste sweeter. Sylvie did it without thinking at dinner at her grandmother's one time, and her grandfather stopped everything to say, "Oh, look at Miss Fancy Pants, now it's salt on the melon?" For the rest of the dinner it was, "Pass Miss Fancy Pants the salt. She'll want it on her pie."

I'd never met any of them. Of course, I was deeply curious to see them. Sylvie and Sam are children of my house, and these were their family. The sad thing was, Rachel and I could have had a really interesting conversation about the one thing we absolutely have in common. It might have helped both of us. But she would never allow it, and I understand. To her I had to be the one who Took Her Life from her, and nothing else, just a cardboard figure for whom a special circle in Hell is waiting.

I sat in the waiting room until early evening. Cell phones didn't work inside the hospital, so I'd go outside to pick up messages and talk to Sam. He was in L.A., and would take the red-eye, be in Boston in the morning.

Sylvia Faithful Mommy's coma was lighter by evening. She was moving more. She squeezed Granma's hand, but not Aunt Lynn's. Lynn took my chair and started a campaign to make Mommy squeeze her hand too. I know Mommy could hear at least some of it, because a little furrow would come between her eyebrows for a moment. I was relieved when Granma said she had to use the little girls' room. Lynn took her away, very solicitous. I suppose to show me how a good daughter acts. I who was to blame for all Mommy's unhappiness. They must have gone down to get supper because I had almost an hour to myself with Mommy. I talked to her. I told her I loved her. I asked her to please come back, I asked her to forgive me if I'd hurt her. I cried. I tried to meditate but the door that so often opens for me was closed. I tried praying to Daddy's god, but that phone was off the hook. I felt like a lamb with its head caught in barbed wire, and no shepherd anywhere. All the shepherds had left the building.

When Granma and Lynn came back, I went out to the waiting room. Nika was doing sudokus. She said she'd reserved a room for us at the Ritz. I said, "Whoa, now I'm really a Miss Fancy Pants." She said, "Might as well be hanged for a sheep as a lamb."

Monica Faithful If you're having an awful day, at least have it in style. They gave us a room with two king-sized beds overlooking the Common, and we both had baths, then ordered dinner from room service and ate in our big white hotel bathrobes. Then we got into our beds and watched a movie. Sylvie called the hospital before going to sleep. Her mother was resting quietly. I called Norman to say good night, and was relieved to hear he'd been checking with the hospital too. He wanted to talk to Sylvie but she shook her head. I said she was already asleep, which she mostly was.

Norman will hit the roof when the bill comes. So be it.

Sylvia Faithful I slept like the dead for about six hours, but woke up early. When I couldn't get back to sleep, I got up and dressed in the bathroom, wrote Monica a note, and got a taxi back to the hospital.

Mommy was alone. There are visiting hours in the ICU but no one pays much attention. And the doctor wanted us to talk to Mommy, to try to get her to wake up. The nurses gowned and gloved me and I went in.

Her arms were tied to the bedrails. I went back out to ask if that was necessary; they said she had pulled out her breathing tube in the night and tried to get the IV out too.

They told me that was good news. When I went back in she was stirring and looked very unhappy, tugging with her wrists. I think something itched and she couldn't scratch. It was horrible. I took her hand and sat; I started talking to her. I tried over and over to get her to open her eyes or say my name. She moved her head back and forth and scowled, but it wasn't at me, it was the restraints. I decided to sing to her. She loved the movie *High Society,* so I sang "True Love," and "What a Swell Party This Is." She got quieter and I think she was listening. I was on the third verse when Sam walked in.

Sam Faithful "This pink champagne, so good for the brain..." I didn't know whether to cry or laugh. Mom looked really awful and she was handcuffed to the bed. After I hugged Sylvie I leaned over Mom and kissed her and said, "Mom, it's Sam. I'm here." She turned her head to me immediately and got one eye partly open. Sylvie sat down and burst into tears.

Monica Faithful That was the breakthrough moment. She was responding, coming out of it. The doctors had been worried about how long she had been out, afraid about brain damage.

I'd heard Sylvie close the door on her way out, and had gotten up and followed to the hospital as soon as I could. I saw Sam for a minute as he came in. Sylvie came to the waiting room to tell me what had happened, that she had responded to Sam.

Lynn and a man with a potbelly and a yarmulke started into the waiting room toward Sylvie; then they saw me, and Lynn grunted and grabbed his elbow and dragged him back out. "Uncle Len," said Sylvie. Rachel's retired brother, up from Florida. It was time for me to go.

I asked her if she would be all right. She said, yes, now that Sam was there. They would stay with their grand-mother and Aunt Lynn, and if that was too hard, she had a credit card of Norman's and could go to a motel. She said they'd be all right, and she promised to call. Since she had her cell phone back, I went out and bought her a charger for it, and brought it to the hospital before I left.

The whole way back to Maine I kept thinking of how many times Sylvie had been the glue that held the family together. The night Edie told us she was dropping out of college, she brought Sylvie with her. Sylvie's a rock. She trusted and actually loved my terrifying mother, which was such a good thing in poor Sydney's life. And what do I do? I forget to call her when we decided to scatter the f-ing ashes. Whether she could have gotten there or not, I could have called her.

You're never too old to keep failing your children, are you? Why weren't we told this was a life sentence?

Jimmy Moss Monica only stayed long enough to pack the car when she got back from Boston. Eleanor gave the last family dinner when all three of us would be together, and that was a welcome diversion from the rolling Charlesie crisis. Nika left the next morning to drive home, and Joss moved us all into the front bedrooms, which pleased her. Regis immediately fell down the front stairs and broke a front tooth. He swore someone had pushed him, though he'd been alone up there. It wasn't the ghost of Uncle

George; he smokes cigars and flushes the toilets, but he never does anything to children. Mother, is that you?

Eleanor Applegate I was disgusted with Charlesie. He was supposed to write two papers this summer and read *Moby-Dick,* and he hadn't done any of it. Ever since he and Mutt won the Retired Skippers' Race, he's been running with the Dodge grandchildren, out till all hours and having parties on the club bathing beach that keep the neighbors up half the night. And which, after all, is private property, for members only. He thinks he's made new friends; I think they're using him and it's an excuse for all of them to drink all night. Jimmy reminded me that when he was that age, Papa sent him to Denmark for a summer to work on a pig farm. He recommended it. I thought he was kidding, but he wasn't.

Josslyn Moss I was finally able to give the kind of party *I* like in my own house, for *our* friends, without all the old china and the octogenarians. They're not that much older than me, but Jimmy's sisters are really another generation. At our party we had crab rolls on paper plates, and hot dogs for the kids, and a contest for spitting watermelon seeds and a blanket toss on the lawn, and everyone went home by nine o'clock. The kids loved it. I loved it.

Jimmy Moss Being under the same roof with my sisters, especially at Leeway—nothing else means home in quite the same way. I was sorry Nika had left. The lower meadow was full of fireflies, and the meteor showers had begun. I believe we saw the northern lights there a couple of times when we were little, but I don't trust my memory. Nika would know.

I'd love for the kids to see them, if it's not a false memory altogether.

Sam came up for Labor Day weekend. His mother was
out of the hospital. He taught Virgil to play cribbage and
we all went to the fair. Looking for Charlotte and Wilbur
in the livestock barn. Sam left, driving a car across country
for Rufus Maitland, and taking our puppy home. Joss and I
had a September sail by ourselves. You get up one morning
and there's a certain kind of edge to the chill, and it's fall.
September is the most beautiful month of the year in
Dundee. The bay was suddenly empty, the breeze was light
and the air was pink and gold on the water.

Someone wrote to me when our parents died that no
one ever tells you there's something good about being an
orphan. That you own yourself in the universe in a new
way. It's true. And I looked at the silent universe that afternoon, ghosting along the empty water toward home, and I
absolutely loved the world.

Monica Faithful The house was a mess when I got to
Sweetwater. The cleaning lady was on vacation and it
didn't look to me as if Norman had emptied a wastebasket
or run a wash all month. He was out of clean socks but he
thought if he wore dirty ones inside out that took care of it.
He said he'd made a good start on a new book, something
about Christ riding the subway, but from what I was hearing he'd been up at the club playing golf with Clark
Vogelsang six days out of seven. It took me three days of
solid work to put the house back in order, not including getting the disposal fixed (one of my grandmother's sterling
egg spoons was in it).

Norman Faithful Well of course I spent some time with Clark Vogelsang. His wife is off at the dry-out bin and he's lonely and upset. In counseling you see it can be devastating to a marriage when one spouse gives up an addiction. The addiction is like a person in the marriage. When it leaves, many times people like what's left less than they liked the addiction. I was trying to talk him through it, get him ready to support Beccy when she gets home.

Monica Faithful I went to school one day to prepare my classroom and guess what. There had been a flood over the summer from the boys' bathroom on the second floor. No one discovered it for days, so the ceiling in my supply closet fell in. It wrecked all the materials that I'd made and collected for twenty years. I came home that night and said to Norman, "Do not tell me that this is really an opportunity. Just frigging do not." And he didn't. But he didn't say much else either.

The next day I was down at the five-and-ten buying construction paper and rolls of felt, when there bearing down on me was Lindsay Tautsch. She asked if I had a minute. Did I look like I had a minute?

She hung around waiting for me to finish my shopping, then we went next door to the Café Express. She bought us some ghastly coffee things with butterscotch sauce and whipped cream. I must not have heard what she said when she asked me if I wanted one. We sat on stools in the window like Betty and Veronica at the Sweet Shoppe, and she told me that she didn't want me to be blindsided. By what? said I.

Well, she said, in that faux-mournful voice of hers, there

was reason to believe that things were not quite right in the church's financials. There were questions about the rector's discretionary fund.

I had no idea what to say. I thought she was just trying to poison every well that Norman drank from. She said yes, she knew I'd be distressed. She said that a member of the vestry, an accountant, had had a look at the books while Norman was in Maine. (Not hard to guess who *that* was.) He'd been wanting to do that for a while, she crooned, because it's a bad sign when someone who keeps the books for an organization never takes a vacation. It often means there's something there he doesn't want anyone else to see.

Or that he's a profoundly dedicated servant of the institution in question, I said. She took my hand, and said, "Let's pray together."

Margaret Sector I'd had my own little visit from young Lindsay Tautsch in July. She was all dressed up in her priest collar and high heels and a skirt too tight for her size, in spite of the fact it was summer and everyone else in town was in shorts. She wanted to tell me that Norman had "control" issues. Honestly, I hate this jargon that the young talk. So he's bossy. Well, I pointed out, he's the boss. Her point was that Mrs. Cherry, the church secretary, isn't up to her standards. I will grant that the bulletin the week before Easter announced "Plam Sunday." But I didn't like her bringing it to me. I may not be Norman's biggest fan, but I do believe in proper channels. And I happen to think he was entirely right to stand by Mrs. Cherry. She's been a good and loyal servant for many years, and it won't kill us to have a typo or two in the bulletin.

Lindsay Tautsch Father Faithful is a very poor delegator, that's one problem. I'm his curate, I could proofread for him. But I didn't go to *Harvard,* my language skills aren't fancy enough for him. Result of that? He did a funeral for Mary Detweiler in June. It went fine. Then Edna Wally died on the Fourth of July (and why her children had a ninety-three-year-old woman out watching the parade in that heat, I don't know) and they asked Norman to do the service. They're Presbyterians but they've worshipped with us since the Reverend Macramé started his hootenanny over there. So Norman told Mrs. Cherry to do Search and Replace on the program from Mary Detweiler's funeral, just change Mary to Edna and Detweiler to Wally, and then *obviously* didn't proof it, because we found ourselves on our knees praying to the Virgin Edna. You wouldn't think it was funny if it was *your* mother's funeral.

Calvin Sector Lindsay Tautsch came to see me the week I got back from Beaumaris. She came to the house with Bill Pafford. I've known Lindsay Tautsch since she was small. Her father was a champion bridge player and a mean drunk. She said that while Father Faithful was away, she had asked Bill to look at the books, because there were things she didn't understand about the church finances. She just wanted to understand. Trying to grow in her job. I tell you the truth, I thought it was smarmy. Not very Christian of me, is it? I pointed out that she should have asked me first, and Bill said they didn't want to bother me on vacation and didn't think I'd mind. Really.

Then Bill told me that he'd found that the rector's

discretionary fund was empty, and that there were unexplained withdrawals from other accounts, especially the building fund. I was disturbed, of course, but I pointed out that the discretionary fund was exactly that—to be used for any purposes the rector deemed worthy, at his discretion. That was a little smarmy of *me,* of course. But there are people in need who come to him in confidence, and we shouldn't breach their trust. I thanked them and said that I'd get back to them. Then I went to Norman.

I was on the search committee that had called Norman to Good Shepherd. He's a marvelous preacher. I knew that he'd be working on his sermon on a Thursday afternoon, and he would know that it wasn't a trifling matter that I chose that time to interrupt him.

We sat in his study window overlooking the church close. I told him there were rumors that needed addressing, sooner rather than later, and that I was calling a special meeting of the vestry. He assured me that he knew about the rumors, but that what we had was a personnel problem. Things were stalled because the bishop was on vacation, but as soon as he was back, he would solve it. I was reassured by his manner, and we talked a little while about what to do. It would be tricky to counsel Lindsay Tautsch to move on, since she grew up here and has her following, but I'd seen enough to believe this might not be the right place for her.

Norman Faithful It was Proper 19 that Sunday, one of my favorites. I decided to use the lesson from Ecclesiasticus. The older I get, the more the Apocrypha interest me. And I would ask the Reverend Tautsch to read the Gospel.

The Gospel reading is from Matthew, about the king

whose servant owes him ten thousand talents. The debtor weeps and begs and the king cancels the debt. Then the debtor runs into a man on the road who owed *him* a hundred denarii, and when the small debtor begs for more time, the big debtor grabs him by the throat and has him thrown into prison. The other servants report this to the king, and the king calls the big debtor a scoundrel and orders him tortured.

Standing in the middle of the church reading that story should be an interesting experience for her.

Monica Faithful Norman asked me to read the lesson. He hasn't asked me to do that for a long time, but it annoys him when some won't conclude a reading from the Apocrypha with "The Word of the Lord," instead of "Here ends the lesson." I'm not getting into the "divinely inspired or not" battle. Unless you want to talk about Swedenborg.

I get terrible stage fright so I have to read the piece over and over before I get into the pulpit. I went around for the rest of the week declaiming it: "Rage and anger, these also I abhor, but a sinner has them ready at hand. Whoever acts vengefully will face the vengeance of the Lord, who keeps strict account of sins."

Calvin Sector The whole vestry was in church that Sunday. I can't say it was a pleasant service; the trio my wife calls "the Unholy Trinity" were back. They'd left us for several months, driving into Pittsburgh every Sunday to worship at an Anglo-Catholic church to express their displeasure that Norman won't use Rite One more than once a month. Well, Norman likes to leave a silent time during the

Prayers of the People for members of the congregation to pray aloud. I didn't think I was going to care for it, but I find that I do; the whole congregation learns that way that someone should be on their prayer lists, or that thanksgiving for a birth or a recovery of health is in order. It gets you out of your own little bubble of concerns, reminds you that we're all part of the body of Christ. Anyway, during the Prayers of the People, the small fat one prayed loudly that our brother Chandler Spring be healed of his drunkenness and homosexuality. You could hear people gasp all over the church. Norman put a fast end to it. He swung right into the General Confession before the other two could chime in and pray for something worse. There was some confusion, people were thrashing through their prayer books, trying to find the right page.

Margaret Sector I was ushering with Chan Spring that day. Blessedly, he'd been outside smoking during the Prayers of the People. He usually takes the left side of our aisle, and I the right, but I made him switch with me, so he wouldn't have to pass the plate to those three.

Goodness, they were pleased with themselves.

Lindsay Tautsch In a church community, the angry, sick, and sad are expressly invited to the table, and of course, they come. I admired the way Father Faithful handled it. I doubt I'd have done as well.

Margaret Sector Remember the time that young man in the mirrored sunglasses was arrested in the middle of the Easter Eucharist?

Calvin Sector At Good Shepherd?

Margaret Sector Doug something. He used to come to the coffee hour and chat up the single ladies? And once he came up to the house and tried to sell you insurance, remember?

Calvin Sector I've forgotten.

Margaret Sector You'll have to forgive my husband. He can't remember anything unpleasant about anybody. It's the way his brain is made, you tell him something ugly and it rolls right into a chute and out the back of his head.

Don't you remember, they led him out the side door in handcuffs?

Calvin Sector How could they do that? Isn't the church a sanctuary?

Margaret Sector That's exactly what you said at the time! At least you're consistent.

Calvin Sector Anyway. The coffee hour was pretty lively that morning, and it was Norman at his best. People were crowding around him. I even saw Lindsay Tautsch give him a hug. The Unholy Trinity appeared briefly, but they caught the sense of the meeting and slunk away.

The vestry went into session right after the Fellowship Hour. Coffee and sandwiches provided by the tireless Bertha Manly, but we hardly needed them. I had not committed an agenda to paper; it seemed to me that it would be

better if there were no record that this meeting ever happened, if it went the way I thought it would, and it did.

The charges were produced. I left that to Frank Heroy,
since he's the treasurer. Rather large withdrawals from the
building fund seemed irregular, and a couple from the fund
to replace the organ, and the fact that the discretionary
fund appeared to have been emptied early in the year, with
no receipts or records.

Norman was absolutely unruffled. He apologized for
worrying us. He said he was guilty of being behind on his
housekeeping chores, but that his records for the discretionary fund would be up-to-date by Wednesday. He had
no idea about the building fund but was perfectly sure
nothing was amiss. He looked me straight in the eye and
said, "You have nothing at all to fear here. Your trust in me
is not misplaced. Be at peace about this." I watched him as
he looked from one of us to the next.

One on one, we had his word.

I said, "That's good enough for me, Norman. Any discussion?"

There was none. The meeting was adjourned twenty
minutes after it started. We all took our sandwiches and
went home.

Letter to Monica Faithful from Rebecca Vogelsang:
October 10
Dear Monica,
First, I want to tell you how much I have admired and
respected you, ever since we first came to Sweetwater. You

have in no way deserved what has happened. If I could change it, I swear I would.

Monica, I know now that I have been in the grip of something much stronger than I am, that I could not change without a tremendous amount of help that I was ashamed to ask for. I am blessed beyond blessed to have been given that help anyway, by my loving family and so many others. But I have a long hard road ahead of me, and I won't get far if I can't admit my manifold faults and try in any way I can to make amends. I can imagine how hurt you are, and it hurts me terribly to think about it. Norman is hurting too, I know, but that was never my affair. What is between husband and wife is for them to take to their Lord. I thank God every hour that I draw breath that my Clark has been willing to stand by me, and I see now that there is still a very powerful bond between you and Norman in spite of everything. I thank God for that too.

I can't undo what has been done, Monica. But I hope you will accept this apology. It comes from the bottom of my heart. I don't ask you to forgive me, but I have a hope that someday you will allow me to embrace you as a sister. And though I have no right to, I do hope that you will be able to forgive Norman. He may have sinned, but it came from a place of goodness. He was trying to help me.

Ever your friend,
Rebecca Vogelsang

Monica Faithful Well, how do you *think* I felt?
All right. Sorry. All right.

The letter arrived on a Thursday. I got home from school about three, put the groceries away, and went out to the hall to sort the mail. When I saw the envelope, I thought, how nice. You hardly ever get a handwritten letter any more.

Well, it came at me in waves. At first I think I shut down. I stared at the letter, seething in my hand, but my brain was scrambling the images.

Then I began to be able to read again. I read it over and over. The way she kept using my name made me want to kill her with my bare hands.

I stayed alone with it for about an hour. I had to adjust. First, to what it meant, and second, to the fact that she clearly thought I already knew. Just assumed, I wonder, dumb as a box of rocks as she is, or had Norman told her he'd confessed?

Norman. Norman Faithful. What on earth had possessed his father to choose a name like that? A little hubris there, don't we think?

Norman. For the previous three weeks, famous Norman Faithful had been in a state, I mean a state, about the accusations against him by Lindsay Tautsch. He wasn't sleeping much, he talked on about how *pilloried* he felt. He had the gall to talk about Christ's suffering, as proof that the Lord would understand and comfort the afflicted, meaning *him*. The vestry had hired an independent auditor to Clear Norman's Good Name, but that didn't seem enough for him. I was surprised he hadn't developed stigmata. And now it all made sense. He was guilty as hell, he'd just been charged with the wrong thing. Waiting for the other shoe to drop.

In school when a child has a tantrum and can't pull out

of it, we tell him to go sit down with his back to the room, take deep breaths, and count to a hundred. Did I do that?

Hell no.

Rosella Cherry It was late on a Thursday afternoon. Mr. Sector was in with Father Norman. Preparing for the vestry meeting on Sunday, I think. The auditors were giving their final report the next day. Monica Faithful marched into the office and barely said hello to me. I started to say he was in a meeting, but she went right by me into the rector's office.

Calvin Sector The door banged open. I thought the church must be on fire. But it was Monica Faithful. She looked from one of us to the other, and I must say, she appeared . . . What's the word I want? *Distrait?*

She didn't say a thing. She took a couple of sheets of pink letter paper out of her jacket pocket, unfolded them, and handed them to Norman. He read. Then he put his head in his hands.

Monica picked up the letter and shoved it at me.

Monica Faithful I don't know how I got through the next few days.

I moved into the guest room that night and stayed there. I'd have left town, but I had a job to go to. It wasn't the school's fault I married an asshole. But staying was like rubbernecking at a car wreck, when it's you in the crumpled heap upside down on the guard rail.

I was so angry at Rebecca Vogelsang, I could barely function. What did she mean, ". . . still a bond between you *in spite of everything*"?

In spite of *what*?

What exactly did he tell her about us? How am *I* supposed to have failed *him*?

And now that we've got this vat of horseradish open, how many have there been?

Can it have started in Oregon? As early as that? There was a particular yummy mummy having a crisis of faith at odd hours, I remember. Certainly in Colorado, there were the adoring Marys and Marthas. And I don't even need to be told who it was in New York. Nor did the awful Bella McChesney.

In seminary, we talked all the time about pastors who use the pulpit as a sexual aid.

So how *could* he?

Norman Faithful I could have explained. I know I could have. I never meant to hurt her. I never meant to hurt anyone. I must have gone to the guest room door four times, five times, in the course of the evening, begging her to come out, just to listen. But she was obdurate. Hard as stone. Even now, I find it hard to forgive her for that.

Margaret Sector Calvin came home with the letter from Beccy Vogelsang. He was shocked that I wasn't shocked.

I was sorry Calvin was head of the vestry. Again. He's seventy-four years old. He doesn't have that many healthy years in front of him. Why does he need this? To have his faith in a friend shattered, to feel that it's *his* fault that Norman Faithful can't keep his pants zipped, or his wallet, that people will blame him, that he blames himself . . . what kind of toll would this take on him? How about on his faith? I'm sick of all of them, Norman, Beccy, Monica, Little Miss Tautsch, all of them.

Calvin Sector What I can't forgive is that he looked us in the eye and lied to us. The whole vestry, one after the other. We were on the line ourselves. I was going around giving people my personal word that the charges were untrue. My personal word.

Margaret Sector My opinion? I don't think he knew he was lying. I think he's one of those people who believes whatever comes out of his own mouth. Think of all the years of standing up above a sea of trusting faces, dressed in shining robes and posing as God's mouthpiece. I've often wondered if Norman believes in anything, except Norman.

Calvin Sector My wife is forgetting how she felt before this broke. They've been dear friends. He's a wonderful preacher.

Margaret Sector I'm not forgetting anything. They've been friends, I've enjoyed their company, and Norman is a wonderful preacher. He's done a lot of socially useful things in his life. But he's got an ego as big as the Ritz, and I never thought he believed in anything. He just went into the family business.

What moral stage is Norman?
    Ah, well, yes. That is the question, isn't it?

❦

Calvin Sector's letter to the congregation of Good Shepherd Episcopal Church:

Dear Fellow Parishioners:

It is with deep regret that we report that the vestry has today accepted Father Faithful's resignation, effective immediately. The Reverend Lindsay Tautsch has agreed to act as interim rector, and we trust that you all will welcome her in her new post, and give her whatever support she needs as she leads us forward at this difficult time.

As some of you know, we have had an outside auditor at work on our books, and her report, which was given to the vestry yesterday morning, will be available in the church office for interested members. Ms. Tautsch will be working with the finance committee to create a new budget for the coming church year and will report to you on the shape of things to come as soon as possible.

We will begin our search for a permanent rector after Christmas. If you know of likely candidates, please communicate with the Search Committee when the time comes; we welcome your input. Until then, be assured that Good Shepherd is strong in trust and love. If you have questions, feel free to be in touch with me, or any member of the vestry.

Yours sincerely,

Calvin Sector, Senior Warden

❦

Lindsay Tautsch You want numbers? Over nine years, just shy of two hundred thousand. Want to know what he did with it? So do we.

Hotels, I'm guessing, with his lady friends. Bespoke clothes he couldn't afford. The Rolex watch, the Italian shoes. Club memberships, his mother's fancy nursing home. He's an awful social climber.

Calvin Sector I don't understand this. It's not even that much money. If he needed it, why didn't he come to me?

Bobby Applegate So that's the way the money goes. Pop goes the weasel.

Calvin Sector He must have been terrified all this time, knowing he'd be found out. It must have been a nightmare for him.

Margaret Sector Oh, Calvin. For heaven's sake.

Monica Faithful The church told me I could stay in the rectory for as long as I needed to after Norman left town, but they were being polite. Norman went off to the dry-out place, the same one Beccy went to, and he had a wonderful time. To this day I don't believe he's an alcoholic, he just needed something to blame besides himself. It was a whole new conversation for him, Norman the fallen, Norman the sinner, whose position is that in Christ, we're all forgiven in advance. He wasn't responsible for anything, it was the *addiction,* the *sickness,* that had screwed all those women and robbed his own church. You know how they say that at AA meetings everyone is laughing and down the hall at the Al Anon meetings, their wives and children are in tears? It's true, and it's not funny.

Oh wait, this part *is* funny. When he decided to go to the dry-out bin, he asked me to pay for it.

By Christmas I had moved into a little apartment down near the river. Near the train tracks, but on the right side of them. (That's a joke.) It was tiny and shoddily built, but clean and fairly new. I hadn't lived alone since the year in Cambridge when Norman was waiting for his divorce. Oh God—Rachel. Would she talk to me now?

I put most of my things in storage. I left Norman's stuff in the rectory; let him deal with it. Let *Mother* Tautsch give it all to the rummage sale.

Jeannie wanted me to get out of town, go to New York, but I had to at least finish the year. This was my town too. I did have my work here, my friends, I was more than the minister's wife.

Oh, that's baloney. I stayed because I was too hurt and angry and addled to make sensible plans. It was a class-B miracle that I could get dressed in the morning and get through my workday. It did mean that I had no effing idea what to do about Christmas, and we do still have children.

In the end, I took Edie and Sylvia to L.A. to be with Jimmy and Josslyn. Their house was full; Josslyn's mother and sister were there. We stayed at a bed-and-breakfast a few blocks from them. Josslyn was lovely about having us all. It was better; her house, her style, her turf. Sam was with us as much as he could be and that was very good for the girls. All three of them were livid at their father.

Sylvia Faithful I admit it. I became a Buddhist to embarrass my father. He was a god to me and it was uncomfortable. But tell me I'm wrong. Buddhism is all about doing away with troublesome ego. How can you go to St. Peter's in Rome and not say that if Jesus walked in here and saw all these statues of dead popes and their marble and gold sarcophagi, he'd think it was demented?

Edith Faithful Someone said Buddhism is better than Christianity because it gets away from the Neolithic craving to gloat over human sacrifice. How about gloating, period?

Josslyn Moss I liked having Monica as a guest. She helped in the kitchen. She asked me how I liked to do things. She taught Boedie to play "Heart and Soul" with her on the piano, and she and Jimmy played some four-hand sheet music they found in the piano bench. Jimmy had only recently started playing again. I guess the music belonged to Aunt Nina.

Monica Faithful We sight-read *Dolly*, the Fauré suite. At least I was sight-reading. Jimmy was doing his part by ear. I caught him when I didn't turn the page in the right place, and he went right on playing. It made me laugh. God, he plays like an angel.

We took long walks in the sun on the Santa Monica pier. I asked Jimmy how Norman could have done what he did. Someone much nicer than I am had told me some elaborate theory that when you're seen as this God-like person but you know that you're human and flawed, you have a need to be found out.

Jimmy listened with that sweet, mild steadiness he has these days, like someone who's been to the moon and knows what it's really made of, but knows it's no use telling the rest of us. He just watches, and helps if he's asked to. So I asked how a man of God, whose whole life is supposed to be a model of goodness, could do what Norman did, and he said, Oh that's easy. Charisma is amoral.

Charisma is amoral. If you have it, you may think at first it's some gift from a higher place that you're supposed to use in a special way, but once you recognize it's much simpler than that, you can do anything you want. And when you see that the world's usual limits don't apply to you, your choices get really interesting.

Bobby Applegate Jimmy called me after Christmas to ask if El would sell her part of Leeway Cottage to him. We had a huge family powwow about it.

Eleanor Applegate The children didn't like it at all. I was surprised at how much they cared. They loved being able to spill over into Leeway when our house is full, the way they could with Monica in it. They clamored about their summer birthdays there, with their grandparents on the porch and the kids playing Capture the Flag in the field below all afternoon. They love those huge family dinners with everyone at one table. Adam and Alison want to be married there.

Bobby Applegate I thought, now wait. Is this a matter of being in love with your own childhood? Change is good. Or change is real. People die. Things end.

Eleanor Applegate I certainly had as many bad memories of that house as good ones. Jimmy probably had the fewest bad ones. And as I said, we wanted to build a guesthouse at the Salt Pond.

Bobby Applegate Of course, Jimmy has the fewest memories of any kind from his childhood, let's be honest. A lot got lost in the fire.

Eleanor Applegate While the subject was on the table, we went to St. Louis. Bobby's nephew was getting married. It was a beautiful wedding. Of course. The children stayed to dance, but Bobby and I went back to our hotel after the cake was cut. Weddings always make me cry, all that youth, all that hope. Bobby carries an extra handkerchief for me at weddings, because I forget I'm going to cry, but he doesn't. At the hotel, there was some sort of wingding going on, a Sweet Sixteen maybe. We were holding hands as we walked through the lobby, and two girls with braces on their teeth, all dressed up, ran after us to the elevator. They said, "Wait— how long have you been married?" We said thirty-six years. "What's the secret?" they wanted to know. (That's when we realized we were holding hands.) I was about to say Never Marry a Man Who Hates His Mother, but Bobby answered first. He said, "Marry someone who makes you laugh, who will never betray you." And he meant me.

A lot has been all my way for a lot of years. So when we got home I asked him what he wanted to do about Leeway, and he said, "Sell to Jimmy." So we did.

Monica Faithful El had told me in February that Jimmy had bought her out and what he'd paid for her share. I waited for him to call about mine. I felt bereft; I mean, I was already so bereft I thought it was going to kill me to lose Leeway too, but life seems to practice an economy of pain. Pile it all on at once, see how long it takes you to snap. I couldn't provide a place where all my children could celebrate Christmas or Hanukkah or the winter solstice together, and now I wouldn't be able to provide a place in the summer either. And I'd felt stretched to breaking *before* that. I couldn't pray. My nights were so long and bleak, I can't tell you. The children would be devastated. I'd failed the three of them in so many ways. How would I keep them together as a family without Dundee? And where would home be for me now?

Josslyn Moss I waited until about March to bring up the subject of Leeway Cottage. I said, "Jimmy, Christmas was fine, but I can't share the house again with your sisters." He said, "I know."

Monica Faithful In early March, Norman's mother died. Died on March Hill, they say in Dundee. They get through Christmas, they even get through February, our old ones, but then March comes and there's still no spring and it's too much to bear. I thought of that, and pictured Hazel, halfway up a hill in patchy snow, with the rocks underfoot glazed with ice and the wind blowing at her baggy skin and her blind old eyes, saying, "No, I've had enough of this." I know she died in her bed at the nursing place, with rails on the sides like a baby's crib, and a glass on her tray of that horrible thickened water that she had to drink because regular water went down the wrong tube and made her choke . . . it's truer to see her splayed out on the path up a hill too steep, having chosen to say, "Stop. I'm done."

Norman called me in tears, to ask me please to come to the funeral. I went, much more for the children than for him. It was a bleak little business in the chapel of the nursing place. Just me and Norman and the three children, and a handful of nurses and of Hazel's most recent friends, in wheelchairs and walkers, probably there more because it was a festive outing for them than because Hazel had made an impression. She'd outlived everybody in her outside world except us. The nurses were very kind, though. They told us stories of happy moments in her last days. They seemed generic, except that one admitted Hazel had been quite exercised about another patient, an old gent who kept wandering into her room and putting his sweater into her drawers.

I guess *that* never ends.

Sylvie went right to the airport and back to New York after the service, but Edie and Sam and I stayed to help Norman pack up Hazel's belongings. We had dinner together, and afterward Norman asked me to sit with him. He talked about what it was like to be sober for the first time in years. He talked about spiritual renewal, and how alone he felt in the world without a church home, without his mother, without me. He cried a lot and apologized a lot.

Eleanor Applegate And of course he asked her to take him back. I said, "Monica, tell me you're not even *thinking* about it." She told me she wasn't. But she was lying.

Jeannie Israel It's very hard to break the habit of trying to make the world right for someone you've loved. It's especially hard if you're a mother, and you've spent decades with those emotional habits of loving and protecting your children. When someone like Norman appeals to those same instincts, it's like turning your back on your best self to say no. Especially if without him, you don't know what you have or who you are. Norman is a genius at understanding that sort of weakness in people.

Monica Faithful Then I got a big envelope from a lawyer in Los Angeles, which said in about thirty-five pages of boilerplate and three sentences I could actually read, that Jimmy had given Leeway Cottage to me.

Josslyn Moss At first I was poleaxed. I said, "Why the hell would you do that? I love that house! The children love that house! Regis has this little ivory elephant he found there that he's carried around with him so much he's broken the tusks off!" Jimmy said, "I thought it would do the greatest good for the greatest number." I said, "I know that's a quote I'm supposed to recognize, asshole."

Jimmy Moss I told her if it made her too unhappy, we wouldn't do it. Nika would give it back.

Josslyn Moss Actually, I knew she would, if we asked.
    Virgil wandered in, and he and Jimmy sat at the piano and sang their new theme song, from some record that came out of our boxes from Connecticut. It's called "Nobody Ever Wants to Court a Warthog." Virgil is starting to play by ear like his dad, and they made me laugh.
    After the kids were in bed, Jimmy said, "Don't forget, something in the house pushed Regis down the stairs." I said, "You don't believe that." He said, "Actually, maybe I do."

I waited for the real reason. Jimmy doesn't like to spell things out, but I wanted more than a ghost story. But I didn't get it.

What are you going to do? I knew what he was like when I married him.

*

An interesting development. Norman has started using a Ouija board. He got the idea from some woman he met at the dry-out place, whom he's keeping company with. He started by wanting to talk to his mother. But instead he's got someone very old and canny, who's given her name as Sarai. She told him Hazel's spirit has already been reborn, to a Mexican mother in Fort Worth. Gave a lot of details about how to find the baby. Didn't go so far as to offer stars to guide him there, but it's enough to keep him busy.

He keeps asking if there's anyone here called Jesus Christ. Sarai gives him puzzle answers. If there were such a being he wouldn't call himself that. If there were such a being he wouldn't be here. That sort of thing. To each according to his needs.

Who is here? As I've said. New arrivals, those in transition. And we who are not going anywhere.

It's true that there are many mansions. Very many. And there are some of us who are built to serve. It's what we're made of, it's what we chose. We arrived like the others, but we don't go on. We stay, to help and guide at the moment of maximum confusion.

No. It isn't sad for us. Oh, maybe it is, a little. Was at first. But there are so many compensations. We do have fun.

BIOGRAPHIES OF CONTRIBUTORS

Adam Applegate, son of Eleanor and Bobby Applegate, is twenty-nine. He attended the University of North Carolina at Chapel Hill, then law school at University of Virginia. He currently practices tax law in Washington, D.C., at the firm of O'Melveny & Myers. He is learning to cook Chinese food, which he especially enjoys because of all the manly chopping with big sharp knives.

Annabelle Applegate, known as Annie, is the oldest child of Eleanor and Bobby Applegate. She is thirty-two. She went to Middlebury College, where she majored in French. She manages the office of a Boston architect and belongs to the Junior League of Boston and to her mother's Topics Club, which she particularly enjoys. She is most proud of having finished the Boston Marathon in under four hours, and would like to live in France for a year.

Bobby Applegate married Eleanor Moss in 1964. An investment banker, president and CEO of Applegate Brothers, Ltd., where he feels only slightly under the thumb of the chairman of the board, his older brother Terry. He grew up in Rye, New York, and graduated from Georgetown. Can play guitar, banjo, and trombone, and still sometimes regrets that he never tried to make it playing rock and roll. John is his favorite Beatle.

Henrik Charles Applegate, called Charlesie, youngest child of Bobby and Eleanor Applegate, is almost nineteen. He has spent a lot of time in the Opportunity Room at school, and couldn't do math if you put a gun to his head, but he can read the wind on the bay like a private language. He would like to be a professional sailor and crew in an America's Cup, and also to sail in the Whitbread Round the World Race. If he can manage to finish high school, he hopes to go to the Maine Maritime Academy in Castine.

Eleanor Wells Moss Applegate, oldest daughter of Laurus and Sydney Moss, was born in Dundee, Maine, in August of 1942. She eloped with Bobby Applegate during her senior year at Skidmore. She completed a master's degree in history of art, hoping to go into museum work, but in the end settled for a lot of volunteering. She particularly likes the following cultural truism: What's the ultimate status symbol? Answer: four kids and a wife who doesn't work. She hopes she can talk her husband into working less and traveling more once Charlesie goes to college. She would like to spend an entire week in the Scuola Grande di San Rocco in Venice, and another in the Prado in Madrid. She is especially proud of her Topics Club, which she keeps on the straight and narrow in spite of the tendency of some of the older members to pay Harvard students to write their Topics papers.

Nora Marion Applegate, younger daughter of Eleanor and Bobby Applegate, just turned twenty-one. As a girl she was passionate about competitive horse show jumping, which she was forced to give up when her mother refused to spend her life trailing around to horse shows from Boston to Florida. She will graduate from Brown with a degree in English literature and would like to live in New York City or San Francisco, or to go to the Iowa Writers' Workshop or else film school. She is also interested in journalism. Biggest unrealized dream: to disguise herself as a boy and ride a racehorse like Elizabeth Taylor in *National Velvet*. Also, she plans to finish the family photo archive she's putting on DVD for everyone as soon as she can get to it.

Trinny Biggs, Sandusky, Ohio. Manager, Second Acts, a store for lightly used children's clothing. Formerly a home-maker in Sand Hills, Oregon. Currently supervising care for her elderly parents. Proudest accomplishment: winning second prize in the local newspaper's biannual quilt contest for her original appliqué pattern quilt called Hawaiian Luau. She would like to visit Honolulu.

Benedikte Bastlund is a lawyer in Copenhagen. Mar-ried to Iain McCallum, a Scottish professor of maths. They have three grown children, all living in Denmark. Her fa-vorite pastime: golf vacations in Scotland.

Alison Boyd grew up in New York City, partly raised by her grandmother when her mother became ill. She grad-uated from Wheaton College and is currently working at the Renwick Gallery in Washington, D.C. She met Adam Applegate at a wedding in Richmond. Her proudest accom-plishment: she overcame her fear of flying and went skydiving. Once. She especially likes summer storms in Washington, when the sky turns purple-green.

Kendra Brayton is retired. She lives with her husband in a gated senior community in Orange County, California. She enjoys visiting her grandchildren. She swims fifty laps in the pool at least four times a week, and walks briskly with two girlfriends on the other days. She has organized progressive dinner parties where you have a different course at each person's house, and enjoys a trip to Las Vegas twice a year. Her favorite first lady was Barbara Bush.

Owen Cantwell is long retired, but his firm keeps an office for him and he goes in every day. He counsels the young associates, though more and more they seem to him like children masquerading as lawyers. He and his wife have passed their sixty-fifth anniversary. He can see and she can hear, which works out pretty well. He is too old to have a favorite Beatle but believes you would have to go a long way to do better than the score of *Oklahoma!*

Rosella Cherry lives in Sweetwater, Pennsylvania. Grew up in Aliquippa, Pennsylvania, daughter of a steel worker. Briefly married, has one daughter living in Australia, who is an otologist. She was the longtime one-woman sales force for the town's only bookstore, now defunct. Retrained for office work at a local business college and is now church secretary at Good Shepherd Episcopal. She also sings first alto in the choir. Paul is her favorite Beatle.

Lincoln Cluett is a Philadelphia lawyer. He met his wife Janet at a glee club dance at Miss Pratt's School, when his friend Eleanor Moss put him on Janet's dance card. He plays championship bridge and has recently taken up croquet. Biggest thrill to date: a trip to Gambia to visit their youngest daughter who was studying drumming.

Kim Colwin is a Trusts and Estates lawyer in Detroit. He has one daughter at the Stanford Business School and one special-needs son, and is deeply proud of them both. He wears the same pants size he did in college, plays in a seniors squash league, and also enjoys playing mixed doubles tennis with his wife. John is his favorite Beatle. His favorite song is "In My Life."

Syl Conary manages the yacht club in Dundee in the summer and teaches carpentry at the academy in the winter. He enjoys saying that he took the train to New York City once, but there was so much going on at the depot he never did get to see the village.

Toby Crane is the son of Gladdy and Neville Crane, grew up in Philadelphia and spent summers in Dundee, Maine, as a boy. A schoolteacher and confirmed bachelor living in San Rafael, California.

Auggie Dodge was born in Dundee, Maine. Finished high school in Dundee, then did three years in the navy, where he was stationed in Honolulu. Went to work as a finish carpenter in East Dundee Boat Yard in 1963, and took the yard over from Junior Horton in 1985, when Junior retired. His favorite beetle is the sow bug.

Shirley Eaton was born in Union, Maine. Makes breads, rolls, and pizza for Abbott's market in Dundee during the winter; in summer cooks for the family at Leeway Cottage. She grew deeply fond of Sydney and Laurus Moss, and even went down to visit them in Connecticut one winter, to see where they lived the rest of the time. She would like to fly in an airplane to Florida and take her grandchildren to Disney World.

Edith Faithful, known as Edie or Edes, daughter of Monica and Norman, is twenty-two. After a case of mononucleosis, she dropped out of Oberlin, where she had been studying voice. She is now attending the Culinary Institute in Hyde Park, New York. She would love to go into business with her sister Sylvie. At the moment her favorite singers are Carolyn Mark and Caitlin Cary, her favorite book is *Human Croquet* by Kate Atkinson, and her unrealized ambition is to someday see Tibet.

Monica Moss Faithful, daughter of Laurus and Sydney Moss, was born after her father returned from the war. Called Nika (NEEka) by her family. She graduated from Sarah Lawrence College and married Norman Faithful in 1971. She is an elementary school teacher. Paul was her favorite Beatle, but she can't listen to any Beatle music any more as she knows it all by heart. Her favorite album is *69 Love Songs* by Magnetic Fields, her favorite song is "Hallelujah" by Leonard Cohen, or maybe "Alexandra Leaving." Her favorite book, not counting Austen, Dickens, or L. Frank Baum, is *The Book of Ebenezer Le Page* by G. B. Edwards. She hopes that her proudest moment is still ahead of her. Thanks for asking.

Norman Faithful was born in Carmel, Indiana. He graduated from De Pauw University, then from Harvard Law in 1970. Ordained an Episcopal priest in 1976. He reads little fiction, and likes the triumphal hymns of Easter best. Biggest unrealized ambition: to see Qumran, where the Dead Sea Scrolls were found.

Sam Faithful, son of Norman and Rachel Cohen Faithful, was born in Indiana in 1966. Currently working in Hollywood as a lighting designer. He loves the climate in Southern California, enjoys hang gliding, and does not want to direct. He is interested in kabbalah and also in the Sufi poet Rumi. His favorite book is anything by Neil Gaiman. He plays a mean game of snooker.

Sylvia Faithful, daughter of Norman and Rachel Cohen

Faithful, was born in Cambridge, Massachusetts, and is thirty-two. Worked her way through the New School waiting on tables. Currently running the room at a new restaurant in west SoHo, and moonlighting as catering waiter/bartender. She can't imagine living anywhere but New York, and her favorite thing about the restaurant business is playing liar's poker at the bar with the rest of the staff after they close for the night. On her favorite playlists are Sam Lardner, especially *Barcelona,* and also the New Pornographers and Goldfrapp.

Homer Gantry. Childhood summer friend of Sydney Brant Moss. Once worked briefly in the insurance industry, but found that he was not for it and it was not for him. For many years was a trustee and chief source of funds for Ischl Hall, the renowned summer music school in Dundee, Maine. Now lives in winter with his wife Gloria in Rosemont Village in Philadelphia, a retirement community. In summer, his three children return their parents to their cottage on Carleton Point in Dundee, where they are attended by a live-in "housekeeper," in charge of balancing their prescription medicines and their alcohol intake, and driving. His favorite composer is Schubert, but he likes to tell people it's Ethelbert Nevin.

Ellen Gott was born in Dundee, Maine, in 1917. Long-time summer cook and housekeeper for the Moss family at Leeway Cottage, she retired in 1986. She stayed in touch with Mr. and Mrs. Moss, and always kept them supplied with butterscotch cookies that no one could get right but her. She can no longer see to drive but can bake from touch and habit. She does laugh about the Thanksgiving when she made the apple pies with cayenne pepper instead of cinnamon. She enjoys getting out for a drive and going to the

Baptist Church with her granddaughter on Sundays. Eleanor Applegate sends her the large print edition of the *New
York Times,* and she enjoys some, but not all, of the books on
tape she gets from the library.

Elise Maitland Henneberry. Childhood summer friend
of Sydney Brant Moss, Gladdy McClintock Crane, Homer
Gantry, and their crowd. "Aunt Elise" to all the young in
the summer community. A legendary fund-raiser for many
New York institutions, including New York Hospital, the
City Ballet, and the New York Public Library. She and her
husband divide their time between Park Avenue and their
house in East Dundee. They keep scrupulous count of the
days they spend outside of New York so they can pay taxes
and vote in Maine. She enjoys gardening, watching her
grandchildren's sailing races, and rereading books she loved
in her youth like *The Forsyte Saga* and *The Winthrop Woman.*
She has no unrealized ambitions. She's had a blessed life.

Jeannie Courtemanche Israel. Monica Moss's best friend
in life since they met at age eight in summer sailing class in
Dundee and neither one could tie a bowline. A psychothera-
pist in New York City, fifty-three. Married, no children. Unrealized ambition: to be a fearless old lady sitting on the
porch of Leeway Cottage with Monica and Amelia, thump-
ing their canes and terrorizing the young. Her husband was
recently diagnosed with multiple sclerosis, but they are both
still hoping to travel when she retires. She would like to see
Antarctica and has recently begun learning Italian.

Betty Kersey. Formerly a homemaker, mother, and rector's wife, she now works as an event planner in Mountain
View, California. She stays in touch with old friends from

their church days by e-mail, including Monica Faithful. Her guilty secret: that she loves computer games like Myst and Riven, and don't even talk to her about computer solitaire. Current peeve about her job: fund-raising affairs where they auction off a puppy at the end. Someone with a snootful always buys it even though his wife is holding his arm down, and two days later, they give it back and guess who has to find a home for it.

George Kersey. Curate in same county as Norman in Missouri in the seventies. Served in several parishes before becoming rector of St. Jude's in Mountain View, California. Served for eight years before leaving the profession to become a school business manager. After some initial difficulty coming to grips with bookkeeping on computer, he enjoys his job and loves the bustle of school. He prefers to worship in private. His favorite writer is C. S. Lewis. Guilty secret: he loves Oprah.

Carla Lowen. Currently a professor of medieval history at Vassar, she shares a cottage with Alice Dubey, head librarian at the college. She enjoys wearing the saris Alice has given her and taught her how to drape. Guilty secret: she still smokes, but only on the back porch overlooking the asparagus beds, as Alice won't let her do it in the house.

Rufus Maitland was born in 1940 in New York City. After Yale he served in Southeast Asia, where he learned Vietnamese and a smattering of Mandarin. He has sailed all over the world and enjoys practicing his language skills via ham radio. Things his friends would be surprised to learn about him: he knows how to read palms, and can play the harp.

Selina Malecki, wife of the bishop of New Hampshire. A wife, mother, and hostess. She enjoys researching her family tree online and that of her husband. She has a special-needs grandson with whom she spends a great deal of time so her daughter can run her business, a plant nursery and garden center. She enjoys figure skating in winter and works part-time as a reading specialist at the local public school. Her hobby is extreme knitting.

Bella McChesney grew up in Buffalo. She was a dance instructor before her marriage, and still does a flashy tango. She has three grown stepchildren and a daughter just now applying to colleges. Hobbies: embroidery and cooking. She belongs to three book groups and enjoys choral singing. Proudest accomplishment: persuaded her husband to go to Couples Week at the Golden Door, where he finally tried yoga, and loved it.

Paul McChesney is a sixth-generation New Yorker. He made his living in advertising. He belongs to the Knickerbocker Club, the Princeton Club, and the Coffee House, where he spends many daytime hours, as his wife made clear when he retired that she had married him for better or worse but not for lunch. He serves on the board of the New York City Opera, the Village Community School, the Kips Bay Boys Club, and the vestry of Holy Innocents.

Amelia Crane Morriset, daughter of Gladdy and Neville Crane. She was a childhood summer friend of Eleanor and Monica Moss, and Sydney Moss's goddaughter. Married to Tommy Morriset, an architect, and lives in Los Gatos, California. She has three grown children, Barbara, Sarah, and Henry. No grandchildren yet. Her secret ambition is to join the Peace Corps.

Boedicia Moss (BOE-di-SEE-a), daughter of Jimmy and Josslyn Moss, is currently seven years old. She used to love the *Teletubbies,* but doesn't any more. Posh is her favorite Spice Girl. She is the best in her class at spelling. She would like to be famous, either a movie star or a rock star. She would also like to be a teacher.

James Lee Moss, known as Jimmy. Youngest child of Laurus and Sydney Moss. He is the chief creative officer of a computer game company that will go public next year, and is fond of quoting his brother-in-law Bobby, saying that he is the only person who could parlay a career out of years on psychedelic drugs. He regrets that he still cannot read music, but very little else.

Josslyn Berry Moss grew up in Orinda, California, and just had her fortieth birthday. She met Jimmy in L.A. at a meditation intensive. She is a mother of three, plays championship tennis, and does either yoga or Pilates five times a week. She is also a triple Pisces, and has recently discovered Montana.

Regis Moss, second son and middle child of Jimmy and Josslyn Moss, is eight and three-quarters. He enjoys soccer and kung fu and his best friend is named Omar. Favorite *Star Wars* character: Luke Skywalker. Pet peeve: his sister because she keeps playing with his Transformers and losing pieces. He doesn't like piano lessons. He would like to be a Jedi Knight.

Virgil Moss, oldest son of Jimmy and Josslyn Moss, is ten years old and just got glasses. Plans to be a biologist. He has an aquarium with three turtles, and when he is twelve he will be allowed to get tropical fish. Pet peeve: his mom makes him let Regis play with him and his friends and

Regis can't catch, and also he cries. He will also be a race car driver. His friend Jason has a trampoline.

Frannie Ober, b. 1947. Daughter of Hannah Gray and Ralph Ober. Grew up in Boston, but spent summers in Dundee, at her parents' camp on Second Pond. She attended Smith College, where she was active in protesting the Vietnam War. She moved to Portland, Maine, after college, but continued to spend summers in Dundee. On a dare she ran for the state house of representatives when she was still in her twenties, and won. Currently serving her second term in Washington, D.C., as a U.S. congresswoman. She is married with two children, both in college.

Al Pease. Longtime chief of Volunteer Fire Department and poker buddy of Laurus Moss. Married to Cressida Dodge. Still losing his battle to become retired from Dundee Plumbing and Heating, which he runs with his son Jeff.

Cressida Pease has spent her whole life in Dundee, with the exception of two years at Husson College. Has recently retired from Ronnie's Hair Care, but she still keeps the books for the family plumbing and heating company. She wishes her grandchildren didn't live so far away, and she misses the days when the summer people left in September and didn't come back until June.

Jeff Pease, b. in Dundee. Completed high school at the Academy in Dundee and would like you to know he escorted Congresswoman Frannie Ober to her first dance, at the Hanger over in Trenton, Maine. He joined the navy and spent two years in Vietnam. When allowed, he came straight home, married Patty Haskell, and joined his father in Plumbing and Heating.

Leonard Rashbaum. A litigator and senior partner at O'Melveny & Myers in Washington, D.C. He is a widower with four children, three in college and one to go, and therefore will not be able to retire until he is 102. He is most proud of having worked pro bono on the team under John Keker that prosecuted Oliver North.

Marta Rowland is currently between husbands, and between her home in New York City and an apartment on the Île St. Louis in Paris, France. She has worked as development director at a private school, which she did very badly, having been brought up not to talk about money, and sold Manhattan real estate, which she did very well, having no objection to hearing other people talk about money if they were planning to give her a cut of it. Her proudest moment is having a bit part in the movie of Tom Wolfe's *Bonfire of the Vanities,* playing a Social X-ray. She did her own costumes and makeup.

Calvin Sector. Grew up in Johnstown, Pennsylvania. He moved to Sweetwater when he went to work for Alcoa after Harvard. He rereads all of Shakespeare in rotation every three years, tragedies one year, comedies the next, then histories. He has promised his children he will give up foxhunting when his present horse is too old. So far he has bought his "last" hunter three times.

Margaret Sector has lived all her life in Sweetwater except for four years at Smith College. She is descended from two Signers and one Chief Justice of the Supreme Court. She sits on the boards of Child Health and also of the Bellknap Home for Crippled Children and is proud that she volunteered her children to be among the first human guinea pigs for the Salk polio vaccine.

Cinder Smart lives in Gates Mills, Ohio. She is a devoted subscriber to the Cleveland Symphony and the Playhouse, and a docent at the art museum. She has a rose garden which is at least locally famous, and you can tell by the state of her manicure that she is not the kind of gardener who points and watches while someone else does the yard work. Her children are trying to teach her how to do e-mail.

Bud Shatterman. President of the Kenyon Alumni Association of Colorado. Ran a profitable GM dealership for many years, and served twice as head of the vestry at St. John's Episcopal Church. He recently lost his wife after her long battle with cancer. He still skis the double diamond slopes, and enjoys his Romeo lunch group (Retired Old Men Eating Out). He is considering signing up for a singles cruise if he can figure out what to wear.

Lindsay Tautsch moved to Sweetwater when she was ten years old. She enjoys bowling and swears her cat Mame was a dog in a former life. She can't imagine more rewarding work than the priesthood. She looks forward to revamping the Inquirers' Classes at Good Shepherd, and hopes to institute a program of organ concerts to reach out to those in the valley who do not yet have a church home.

Clara Thiele still serves on the altar guild at St. John's. She suffered a minor stroke two years ago, from which she fully recovered and is otherwise healthy and counting her blessings. She is planning to take her grandchildren on a trip to discover their Danish roots next summer, and will probably travel on to Moscow and St. Petersburg. She has always wanted to see the Hermitage.

Sandra Thiele, daughter of Clara and George Thiele. Has fallen away from the church and is grateful she and her mother have agreed not to talk about it. She has recently finished her master's in social work and is completing her supervised training; she hopes to open her own family counseling practice by next year.

Rebecca Voglesang is "over forty but barely." She has three children at Sweetwater Academy, the oldest due to graduate this year. She works part-time at the Sweetwater Arts Center, teaches Sunday school, and has taken up horseback riding to keep her youngest company.

Ted Wineapple. Archdeacon of California in San Francisco. A seminary classmate of Norman Faithful, he has served several dioceses in his career. He enjoys the climate in the Bay Area, has twice completed the S.F.-to-L.A. bike ride to benefit HIV/AIDS research, and has sworn not to take up golf until he retires.

ACKNOWLEDGMENTS

Jerri Witt, a dear friend and brilliant pianist, has been a trusted reader of early drafts for me for over a decade, not to mention her heroic efforts to teach me to play the piano. I thank her for her generosity, for the depth and breadth of her musical expertise, and for her wisdom about texts and people. Some may recognize that thanks to Jerri, Laurus's ideas about programming owe much to the great Mitsuko Uchida. To her, too, I am grateful.

Others have offered time, information, and keys that opened doors in the characters' brains, or in mine. For such generosity I am grateful to Nion McEvoy, Lauren Belfer, Rita and Kent Johnson, the Venerable Robert N. Willing, the Reverend Robert Cromey, Pat Beard, Shery Kerr, Sarah Auchincloss, Donald E. Jones, Claire Messud, Jonathan Lethem, and William Bunting.

For their thoughtful readings and comments on various drafts of this book I thank Lauren Belfer and Jerri Witt (again), Robin Clements, David Taylor, Emily Forland, and Lucie Semler.

I am especially grateful for the generosity of Diana Hamilton Stockton, Cary Hamilton Twitchell, Ashleigh Hill, Shannon Miles, and Sarah and Michael Sylvester. I owe special thanks for the ingenious contribution of Heather

Frederick, and to Linda Ferrer, for her invaluable expertise and her marvelous eye, and her friendship.

As always, my agent and lifelong friend Wendy Weil has provided advice, cheer, and wise counsel and I'm grateful to have her in my life. I am also grateful to my editor Jennifer Brehl, whose wisdom and support has added so much to this process. Thanks also to Lisa Gallagher, Michael Morrison, and the team at Morrow who do so much for their writers, and do it so well. Thank you, truly.

And last and most, to my darling husband, Robin Clements, who is always the hero of my story.